Praise for the thrillers of

Jack Higgins

DARK JUSTICE

"High-speed narration." —*Publishers Weekly*

BAD COMPANY

"Higgins writes with spare velocity, racing through a complex plot . . . [and] has no equal in the realm of ex-Nazis wreaking havoc. . . . Higgins maintains the suspense and even manages a series of nasty surprises along the way."
—*St. Louis Post-Dispatch*

"Starts off at light speed and quickly goes into warp drive, never easing up on the throttle so that readers never quite catch their breath." —*Stonnington Leader* (Australia)

MIDNIGHT RUNNER

"The fun comes from the wisecracking band of dangerous but bighearted secret soldiers Higgins wheels out to save the world—and his galloping Hollywood-ready pace." —*People*

"Swift and coursing with dark passion . . . as credible and steel-hearted as Higgins's best." —*Publishers Weekly*

EDGE OF DANGER

"This is Higgins near the top of his game . . . another winner." —*Publishers Weekly*

"His 32nd triumphant exercise in keeping readers hugely entertained." —*Los Angeles Times*

"The action is nonstop." —*Minneapolis Star Tribune*

continued

DAY OF RECKONING

"The action is sleek and intensely absorbing, but the supreme pleasure is in those Higgins celebrates—tarnished warriors who value honor over life and who get the job done no matter what the cost." —*Publishers Weekly*

THE WHITE HOUSE CONNECTION

"*The White House Connection* has one heckuva heroine . . . [who] begins a one-woman assassination spree that will keep you turning the pages." —Larry King, *USA Today*

"Masterful . . . a satisfying, suspense-filled book."
—*Roanoke Times & World News*

"[A] page-turning thriller." —*The Indianapolis Star*

THE PRESIDENT'S DAUGHTER

"High-tension action and harrowing twists—Higgins at his best." —*Midwest Book Review*

"A tight story with plenty of action."—*Chattanooga Free Press*

NIGHT JUDGEMENT AT SINOS

"This is one you won't put down." —*The New York Times*

DRINK WITH THE DEVIL

"A most intoxicating thriller." —The Associated Press

"It is Dillon's likeability and the author's adroitness in giving his character the room he needs that make Higgins's novels so readable." —*The Washington Times*

YEAR OF THE TIGER

"Higgins spins as mean a tale as Ludlum, Forsythe, or any of them." —*Philadelphia Daily News*

ANGEL OF DEATH

"Pulsing excitement . . . Higgins makes the pages fly."
—*New York Daily News*

"The action never stops." —*The San Francisco Examiner*

EYE OF THE STORM

Also published as *Midnight Man*

"Heart-stopping . . . spectacular and surprising."
—*Abilene Reporter-News*

"Razor-edged . . . will give you an adrenaline high. It's a winner." —*Tulsa World*

ON DANGEROUS GROUND

"A whirlwind of action, with a hero who can out-Bond old James. It's told in the author's best style, with never a pause for breath." —*The New York Times Book Review*

SHEBA

"When it comes to thriller writers, one name stands well above the crowd—Jack Higgins." —The Associated Press

THUNDER POINT

"Dramatic . . . authentic . . . one of the author's best."
—*The New York Times*

"A rollicking adventure that twists and turns."
—*The San Diego Union-Tribune*

GRAVEYARD SHIFT

"One-hundred-percent-proof adventure."
—*The New York Times*

BROUGHT IN DEAD

"Action-packed, colourful and written by a natural story-teller." —*Sunday Mail* (London)

Titles by Jack Higgins

HELL IS ALWAYS TODAY
BAD COMPANY
MIDNIGHT RUNNER
THE GRAVEYARD SHIFT
EDGE OF DANGER
DAY OF RECKONING
THE KEYS OF HELL
THE WHITE HOUSE CONNECTION
IN THE HOUR BEFORE MIDNIGHT
EAST OF DESOLATION
THE PRESIDENT'S DAUGHTER
PAY THE DEVIL
FLIGHT OF EAGLES
YEAR OF THE TIGER
DRINK WITH THE DEVIL
NIGHT JUDGEMENT AT SINOS
ANGEL OF DEATH
SHEBA
ON DANGEROUS GROUND
THUNDER POINT
EYE OF THE STORM (*also published as* MIDNIGHT MAN)
THE EAGLE HAS FLOWN
COLD HARBOUR
MEMORIES OF A DANCE-HALL ROMEO
A SEASON IN HELL
NIGHT OF THE FOX
CONFESSIONAL
EXOCET
TOUCH THE DEVIL
LUCIANO'S LUCK
SOLO
DAY OF JUDGMENT
STORM WARNING
THE LAST PLACE GOD MADE
A PRAYER FOR THE DYING
THE EAGLE HAS LANDED
THE RUN TO MORNING
DILLINGER
TO CATCH A KING
THE VALHALLA EXCHANGE
THE KHUFRA RUN
A GAME FOR HEROES
THE WRATH OF GOD

Hell Is Always Today

Jack Higgins

THE BERKLEY PUBLISHING GROUP
Published by the Penguin Group
Penguin Group (USA) Inc.
375 Hudson Street, New York, New York 10014, USA
Penguin Group (Canada), 10 Alcorn Avenue, Toronto, Ontario M4V 3B2, Canada
(a division of Pearson Penguin Canada Inc.)
Penguin Books Ltd., 80 Strand, London WC2R 0RL, England
Penguin Group Ireland, 25 St. Stephen's Green, Dublin 2, Ireland (a division of Penguin Books Ltd.)
Penguin Group (Australia), 250 Camberwell Road, Camberwell, Victoria 3124, Australia
(a division of Pearson Australia Group Pty. Ltd.)
Penguin Books India Pvt. Ltd., 11 Community Centre, Panchsheel Park, New Delhi—110 017, India
Penguin Group (NZ), Cnr. Airborne and Rosedale Roads, Albany, Auckland 1310, New Zealand
(a division of Pearson New Zealand Ltd.)
Penguin Books (South Africa) (Pty.) Ltd., 24 Sturdee Avenue, Rosebank, Johannesburg 2196, South Africa

Penguin Books Ltd., Registered Offices: 80 Strand, London WC2R 0RL, England

HELL IS ALWAYS TODAY

A Berkley Book / published by arrangement with the author

PRINTING HISTORY
John Long edition / 1968
Berkley mass-market edition / May 2005

For information, address: The Berkley Publishing Group,
a division of Penguin Group (USA) Inc.,
375 Hudson Street, New York, New York 10014.

ISBN: 0-425-20286-0

BERKLEY®
Berkley Books are published by The Berkley Publishing Group,
a division of Penguin Group (USA) Inc.,
375 Hudson Street, New York, New York 10014.
BERKLEY is a registered trademark of Penguin Group (USA) Inc.
The "B" design is a trademark belonging to Penguin Group (USA) Inc.

PRINTED IN THE UNITED STATES OF AMERICA

10 9 8 7 6 5 4 3 2 1

Prologue

The police car turned at the end of the street and pulled into the kerb beside the lamp. The driver kept the motor running, and grinned at his passenger.

"Rather you than me on a night like this, but I was forgetting. You love your work, don't you?"

Police Constable Henry Joseph Dwyer's reply was unprintable and he stood at the edge of the pavement, a strangely melancholy figure in the helmet and cape, listening to the sound of the car fade into the night. Rain fell steadily, drifting down through the yellow glow of the street lamp in a silver spray and he turned morosely and walked towards the end of the street.

It was just after ten and the night stretched before him, cold and damp. The city was lonely and for special reasons at that time, rather frightening even for an old hand like Joe Dwyer. Still, no point in worrying about that. Another ten months and he'd be out of it, but his hand still moved inside his cape to touch the small two-way radio in his breast pocket, the lifeline that could bring help when needed within a matter of minutes.

He paused on the corner and looked across the square towards the oasis of light that was the coffee stall on the other side. No harm in starting off with something warm inside him and he needed some cigarettes.

There was only one customer, a large, heavily built man in an old trenchcoat and rain hat who was talking to Sam Harkness, the owner. As Dwyer approached, the man turned, calling goodnight over his shoulder and plunged into the rain head down so that he and the policeman collided.

"Steady on there," Dwyer began and then recognised him. "Oh, it's you, Mr. Faulkner. Nasty night, sir."

Faulkner grinned. "You can say that again. I only came out for some cigarettes. Hope they're paying you double time tonight."

"That'll be the day, sir."

Faulkner walked away and Dwyer approached the stall. "He's in a hurry, isn't he?"

Harkness filled a mug with tea from the urn, spooned sugar into it and pushed it across. "Wouldn't you be if you was on your way home to a warm bed on a night like this? Probably got some young bird lying there in her underwear waiting for him. They're all the same these artists."

Dwyer grinned. "You're only jealous. Let's have twenty of the usual. Must have something to get me through the night. How's business?"

Harkness passed the cigarettes across and changed the ten-shilling note that Dwyer gave him. "Lucky if I make petrol money."

"I'm not surprised. You won't get many people out on a night like this."

Harkness nodded. "It wouldn't be so bad if I still had the Toms, but they're all working from their flats at the moment with some muscle minding the door if they've got any sense. All frightened off by this Rainlover geezer."

Dwyer lit a cigarette and cupped it inside his left hand. "He doesn't worry you?"

Harkness shrugged. "He isn't after the likes of me, that's for certain, though how any woman in her right mind can go out at the moment on a night when it's raining beats me." He picked up the evening paper. "Look at this poor bitch he got in the park last night. Peggy Nolan. She's been on the game round here for years. Nice little Irish woman. Fifty if she was a day. Never harmed anyone in her life." He put the paper down angrily. "What about you blokes, anyway? When are you going to do something?"

The voice of the public, worried, frightened and looking for a scapegoat. Dwyer nipped his cigarette and slipped it back into the packet. "We'll get him, Sam. He'll over-reach himself. These nut-cases always do."

Which didn't sound very convincing even to himself and Harkness laughed harshly. "And how many more women are going to die before that happens, tell me that?"

His words echoed back to him flatly on the night air as Dwyer moved away into the night. Harkness watched him go, listening to the footsteps fade and then there was only the silence and beyond the pool of light, the darkness seemed to move in towards him. He swallowed hard, fighting back the fear that rose inside, switched on the radio and lit a cigarette.

* * *

Joe Dwyer moved through the night at a measured pace, the only sound the echo of his own step between the tall Victorian terraces that pressed in on either side. Occasionally he paused to flash his lamp into a doorway and once he checked the side door of a house which was by day the offices of a grocery wholesaler.

These things he did efficiently because he was a good policeman, but more as a reflex action than anything else. He was cold and the rain trickled down his neck soaking into his shirt and he still had seven hours to go, but he was also feeling rather depressed, mainly because of Harkness. The man was frightened of course, but who wasn't? The trouble was that people saw too much television. They were conditioned to expect their murders to be neatly solved in fifty-two minutes plus advertising time.

He flashed his lamp into the entry called Dob Court a few yards from the end of the street hardly bothering to pause, then froze. The beam rested on a black leather boot, travelled across stockinged legs, skirt rucked up wantonly, and came to rest on the face of a young woman. The head was turned sideways at an awkward angle in a puddle of water, eyes staring into eternity.

And he wasn't afraid, that was the strange thing.

He took a quick step forward, dropping to one knee and touched her face gently with the back of his hand. It was still warm, which could only mean one thing on a night like this. . . .

He was unable to take his reasoning any further. There was the scrape of a foot on stone. As he started to rise, his helmet was knocked off and he was struck a violent blow on the back of the head. He cried out, falling across the body of the girl, and someone ran along the entry behind him and turned into the street.

He could feel blood, warm and sticky, mingling with the rain as it ran across his face and the darkness moved in on him. He fought it off, breathing deeply, his hand going inside his cape to the two-way radio in his breast pocket.

Even after he had made contact and knew that help was on its way, he held on to consciousness with all his strength, only letting go at the precise moment that the first police car turned the corner at the end of the street.

1

It had started to rain in the late evening, lightly at first, but increasing to a heavy, drenching downpour as darkness fell. A wind that, from the feel of it, came all the way from the North Sea, drove the rain before it across the roofs of the city to rattle against the enormous glass window that stood at one end of Bruno Faulkner's studio.

The studio was a great barn of a room which took up the entire top floor of a five-storey Victorian wool merchant's town house, now converted into flats. Inside a fire burned in a strangely mediaeval fireplace giving the only light, and on a dais against the window four great shapes, Faulkner's latest commission, loomed menacingly.

There was a ring at the door bell and then another.

After a while, an inner door beyond the fireplace opened and Faulkner appeared in shirt and pants, a little dishevelled for he had been sleeping. He switched on the light and paused by the fire for a moment, mouth widening in a yawn. He was a large, rather fleshy man of thirty whose face carried the habitually arrogant expression of the sort of creative artist who believes that he exists by a kind of divine right. As the bell sounded again he frowned petulantly, moved to the door and opened it.

"All right, all right, I can hear you." He smiled suddenly. "Oh, it's you, Jack."

The elegant young man who leaned against the wall outside, a finger held firmly against the bell push, grinned. "What kept you?"

Faulkner turned and Jack Morgan followed him inside and closed the door. He was about Faulkner's age, but looked younger and wore evening dress, a light overcoat with a velvet collar draped across his shoulders.

He examined Faulkner dispassionately as the other man helped himself to a cigarette from a silver box and lit it. "You look bloody awful, Bruno."

"I love you too," Faulkner said and crossed to the fire.

Morgan looked down at the telephone which stood on a small coffee table. The receiver was off the hook and he replaced it casually. "I thought so. I've been trying to get through for the past couple of hours."

Faulkner shrugged. "I've been working for two days non-stop. When I finished I took the phone off the hook and went to bed. What did you want? Something important?"

"It's Joanna's birthday, or had you forgotten? She sent me to get you."

"Oh, my God, I had—completely. No chance that I've missed the party I suppose?"

"I'm afraid not. It's only eight o'clock."

"Pity. I suppose she's collected the usual bunch of squares." He frowned suddenly. "I haven't even got her a present."

Morgan produced a slim leather case from one pocket and threw it across. "Pearl necklace . . . seventy-five quid. I got it at Humbert's and told them to put it on your account."

"Bless you, Jack," Faulkner said. "The best fag I ever had."

He walked towards the bedroom door and Morgan

turned to examine the figures on the dais. They were life-size, obviously feminine, but in the manner of Henry Moore's early work had no individual identity. They possessed a curious group menace that made him feel decidedly uneasy.

"I see you've added another figure," he said. "I thought you'd decided that three was enough?"

Faulkner shrugged. "When I started five weeks ago I thought one would do and then it started to grow. The damned thing just won't stop."

Morgan moved closer. "It's magnificent, Bruno. The best thing you've ever done."

Faulkner shook his head. "I'm not sure. There's still something missing. A group's got to have balance . . . perfect balance. Maybe it needs another figure."

"Surely not?"

"When it's right, I'll know. I'll feel it and it's not right yet. Still, that can wait. I'd better get dressed."

He went into the bedroom and Morgan lit a cigarette and called to him, "What do you think of the latest Rainlover affair?"

"Don't tell me he's chopped another one? How many is that—four?"

Morgan picked up a newspaper that was lying on a chair by the fire. "Should be in the paper." He leafed through it quickly and shook his head. "No, this is no good. It's yesterday evening's and she wasn't found till nine o'clock."

"Where did it happen?" Faulkner said as he emerged from the bedroom, pulling on a corduroy jacket over a polo neck sweater.

"Not far from Jubilee Park." Morgan looked up and frowned. "Aren't you dressing?"

"What do you call this?"

"You know what I mean."

"Who for, that bunch of stuffed shirts? Not on your life. When Joanna and I got engaged she agreed to take me exactly as I am and this is me, son." He picked up a trenchcoat and draped it over his shoulders. "I know one thing, I need a drink before I can face that lot."

"There isn't time," Morgan said flatly.

"Rubbish. We have to pass The King's Arms don't we? There's always time."

"All right, all right," Morgan said. "I surrender, but just one. Remember that."

Faulkner grinned, looking suddenly young and amiable and quite different. "Scouts' honour. Now let's get moving."

He switched off the light and they went out.

* * *

When Faulkner and Morgan entered the saloon bar of The King's Arms it was deserted except for the landlord, Harry Meadows, a genial bearded man in his mid-fifties, who leaned on the bar reading a newspaper. He glanced up, then folded the newspaper and put it down.

"'Evening, Mr. Faulkner . . . Mr. Morgan."

"'Evening, Harry," Faulkner said. "Two double brandies."

Morgan cut in quickly. "Better make mine a single, Harry. I'm driving."

Faulkner took out a cigarette and lit it as Meadows gave two glasses a wipe and filled them. "Quiet tonight."

"It's early yet," Morgan said.

Meadows pushed the drinks across. "I won't see many tonight, you mark my words." He turned the newspaper towards them so that they could read the headline *Rainlover strikes again*. "Not with this bastard still on the loose. Every time it rains he's at it. I'd like to know what the bloody police are supposed to be doing."

Faulkner swallowed some of his brandy and looked down at the newspaper. "The Rainlover—I wonder which bright boy dreamed that one up."

"I bet his editor gave him a fifty-pound bonus on the spot."

"He's probably creeping out at night every time it rains and adding to the score personally, just to keep the story going." Faulkner chuckled and emptied his glass.

Meadows shook his head. "It gives me the shakes, I can tell you. I know one thing . . . you won't find many women on the streets tonight."

Behind them the door swung open unexpectedly and a young woman came in. She was perhaps nineteen or twenty and well made with the sort of arrogant boldness about the features that many men like, but which soon turns to coarseness. She wore a black plastic mac, a red mini-skirt and knee-length leather boots. She looked them over coolly, unbuttoning her coat with one hand, then sauntered to the other end of the bar and hoisted herself on to a stool. When she crossed her legs, her skirt slid all the way up to her stocking tops. She took a cheap compact from her bag and started to repair the rain damage on her face.

"There's someone who doesn't give a damn for a start," Faulkner observed.

Morgan grinned. "Perhaps she doesn't read the papers. I wonder what the Rainlover would do to her?"

"I know what I'd like to do to her."

Meadows shook his head. "Her kind of custom I can do without."

Faulkner was immediately interested. "Is she on the game then?"

Meadows shrugged. "What do you think?"

"What the hell, Harry, she needs bread like the rest of us. Live and let live." Faulkner pushed his glass across. "Give her a drink on me and I'll have a re-fill while you're at it."

"As you say, Mr. Faulkner."

He walked to the other end of the bar and spoke to the young woman who turned, glanced briefly at Faulkner, then nodded. Meadows poured her a large gin and tonic.

Faulkner watched her closely and Morgan tapped him on the shoulder. "Come on now, Bruno. Don't start getting involved. We're late enough as it is."

"You worry too much."

The girl raised her glass and he toasted her back. She made an appealing, rather sexy picture sitting there on the high stool in her mod outfit and he laughed suddenly.

"What's so funny?" Morgan demanded.

"I was just thinking what a sensation there would be if we took her with us."

"To Joanna's party? Sensation isn't the word."

Faulkner grinned. "I can see the look on Aunt Mary's weatherbeaten old face now—the mouth tightening like a dried prune. A delightful thought."

"Forget it, Bruno," Morgan said sharply. "Even you couldn't get away with that."

Faulkner glanced at him, the lazy smile disappearing at once. "Oh, couldn't I?"

Morgan grabbed at his sleeve, but Faulkner pulled away sharply and moved along the bar to the girl. He didn't waste any time in preliminaries.

"All on your own then?"

The girl shrugged. "I'm supposed to be waiting for somebody." She had an accent that was a combination of Liverpool and Irish and not unpleasant.

"Anyone special?"

"My fiancé."

Faulkner chuckled. "Fiancés are only of secondary importance. I should know. I'm one myself."

"Is that a fact?" the girl said.

Her handbag was lying on the bar, a large and ostentatious letter G in one corner bright against the shiny black plastic. Faulkner picked it up and looked at her enquiringly.

"G for . . . ?"

"Grace."

"How delightfully apt. Well, G for Grace, my friend and I are going on to a party. It occurred to me that you might like to come with us."

"What kind of a party?"

Faulkner nodded towards Morgan. "Let's put it this way. He's dressed for it, I'm not."

The girl didn't even smile. "Sounds like fun. All right, Harold can do without it tonight. He should have been here at seven-thirty anyway."

"But you weren't here yourself at seven-thirty, were you?"

She frowned in some surprise. "What's that got to do with it?"

"A girl after my own heart." Faulkner took her by the elbow and moved towards Morgan who grinned wryly.

"I'm Jack and he's Bruno. He won't have told you that."

She raised an eyebrow. "How did you know?"

"Experience . . . mostly painful."

"We can talk in the car," Faulkner said. "Now let's get moving."

As they turned to the door, it opened and a young man entered, his hands pushed into the pockets of a hip-length tweed coat with a cheap fur collar. He had a narrow white face, long dark hair and a mouth that seemed to be twisted into an expression of perpetual sullenness.

He hesitated, frowning, then looked enquiringly at the girl. "What gives?"

Grace shrugged. "Sorry, Harold, you're too late. I've made other arrangements."

She took a single step forward and he grabbed her arm. "What's the bloody game?"

Faulkner pulled him away with ease. "Hands off, sonny."

Harold turned in blind rage and swung one wild punch that might have done some damage had it ever landed. Faulkner blocked the arm, then grabbed the young man's hand in an aikido grip and forced him to the ground, his face remaining perfectly calm.

"Down you go, there's a good dog."

Grace started to laugh and Harry Meadows came round the bar fast. "That's enough, Mr. Faulkner. That's enough."

Faulkner released him and Harold scrambled to his feet, face twisted with pain, something close to tears in his eyes.

"Go on then, you cow," he shouted. "Get out of it. I never want to see you again."

Grace shrugged. "Suit yourself."

Faulkner took her by the arm and they went out laughing. Morgan turned to Meadows, his face grave. "I'm sorry about that."

Meadows shook his head. "He doesn't change, does he, Mr. Morgan? I don't want to see him in here again—okay?"

Morgan sighed helplessly, turned and went after the others and Meadows gave some attention to Harold who stood nursing his hand, face twisted with pain and hate.

"You know you did ask for it, lad, but he's a nasty piece of work that one when he gets started. You're well out of it. Come on, I'll buy you a drink on the house."

"Oh, stuff your drink, you stupid old bastard," Harold said viciously and the door swung behind him as he plunged wildly into the night.

2

Detective Sergeant Nicholas Miller was tired and it showed in his face as he went down the steps to the tiled entrance hall of the Marsden Wing of the General Infirmary. He paused to light a cigarette and the night sister watched him for a moment before emerging from her glass office. Like many middle-aged women she had a weakness for handsome young men. Miller intrigued her particularly for the dark blue Swedish trenchcoat and continental raincap that gave him a strange foreign air which was hardly in keeping with his profession. Certainly anything less like the conventional idea of a policeman would have been hard to imagine.

"How did you find Mr. Grant tonight?" she asked as she came out of her office.

"Decidedly restless." Miller's face was momentarily illuminated by a smile of great natural charm. "And full of questions."

Detective Superintendent Bruce Grant, head of the city's Central C.I.D., had been involved in a car accident earlier in the week and now languished in a hospital bed with a dislocated hip. Misfortune enough considering that Grant had been up to his ears in the most important case of his career. Doubly unfortunate in that it now left in sole charge of the case Detective Chief Superintendent George Mallory of Scotland Yard's Murder Squad, the expert his superiors had insisted on calling in, in response to the growing public alarm as the Rainlover still continued at large.

"I'll tell you something about policemen, Sister," Miller said. "They don't like other people being brought in to handle things that have happened on their patch. To an old hand like Bruce Grant, the introduction of Scotland Yard men to a case he's been handling himself is a personal insult. Has Mallory been in today, by the way?"

"Oh yes, but just to see Inspector Craig. I don't think he called in on Superintendent Grant."

"He wouldn't," Miller said. "There's no love lost there at all. Grant's one satisfaction is that Craig was in the car with him when the accident happened which leaves Mallory on his own in the midst of the heathen. How is Craig?"

"Poorly," she said. "A badly fractured skull."

"Serves him right for coming North."

"Now then, Sergeant, I was a Londoner myself twenty years ago."

"And I bet you thought that north of High Barnet we rolled boulders on to travellers as they passed by."

He grinned wickedly and the night sister said, "It's a change to see you smile. They work you too hard. When did you last have a day off?"

"A day? You must be joking, but I'm free now till six a.m. As it happens, I've had an invitation to a party, but I'd break it for you."

She was unable to keep her pleasure at the compliment from showing on her pleasant face and gave him a little push. "Go on, get out of it. I'm a respectable married woman."

"In that case I will. Don't do anything I would." He smiled again and went out through the swing doors.

She stood there in the half-light, listening to the sound of the car engine dwindle into the distance, then turned with a sigh, went back into her office and picked up a book.

Nick Miller had met Joanna Hartmann only once at a dinner party at his brother's place. The circumstances had been slightly unusual in that he had been in bed in his flat over the garage block at the rear of the house when his brother had arrived to shake him back to reality with the demand that he get dressed at once and come to dinner. Miller, who had not slept for approximately thirty hours, had declined with extreme impoliteness until his brother indicated that he wished him to partner a national television idol who had the nation by the throat twice-weekly as the smartest lady barrister in the game. It seemed that her fiancé had failed to put in an appearance, which put a completely different complexion on the whole thing. Miller had got dressed in three minutes flat.

The evening had been interesting and instructive. Like most actresses, she had proved to be not only intelligent, but a good conversationalist and for her part she had been intrigued to discover that her host's handsome and elegant younger brother was a policeman.

A pleasant evening, but nothing more, for a considerable amount of her conversation had concerned her fiancé, Bruno Faulkner the sculptor, who had followed her north when she had signed to do her series for Northern Television and Nick Miller was not a man to waste his time up blind alleys.

Under the circumstances her invitation was something of a surprise, but it had certainly come at the right moment. A little life and laughter was just what he needed. Something to eat, a couple of stiff drinks and then home to bed or perhaps to someone else's? You never knew your luck where show people were concerned.

She had the top flat in Dereham Court, a new luxury block not far from his own home and he could hear cool music drifting from a half-open window as he parked the green Mini-Cooper and went up the steps into the hall.

She opened the door to him herself, a tall, elegant blonde in a superb black velvet trouser suit who looked startlingly like her public image. When she greeted him, he might have been the only person in the world.

"Why, Nick, darling, I was beginning to think you weren't going to make it."

He took off his coat and cap and handed them to the maid. "I nearly didn't. First evening off for a fortnight."

She nodded knowingly. "I suppose you must be pretty busy at the moment." She turned to the handsome greying man who hovered at her elbow, a glass in one hand. "Nick's a detective, Frank. You'll know his brother, by the way. Jack Miller. He's a director of Northern Television. This is Frank Marlowe, my agent, Nick."

Marlowe thawed perceptibly. "Why, this is real nice," he said with a faint American accent. "Had lunch with your brother and a few people at the Midland only yesterday. Let me get you a drink."

As he moved away, Joanna took Miller's arm and led him towards a white-haired old lady in a silver lamé gown who sat on a divan against the wall watching the world go by. She had the face of the sort of character actress you've seen a thousand times on film and television and yet can never put a name to. She turned out to be Mary Beresford, Joanna's aunt, and Miller was introduced in full. He resisted an insane impulse to click his heels and kiss the hand that she held out to him, for the party was already turning out to be very different from what he had imagined.

That it was a very superior sort of soirée couldn't be denied, but on the whole, the guests were older rather than younger, the men in evening wear, the women exquisitely gowned. Certainly there were no swinging young birds from the television studios in evidence—a great disappointment. Cool music played softly, one or two couples were dancing and there was a low murmur of conversation.

"What about the Rainlover then, Sergeant Miller?" Mary Beresford demanded.

The way she said sergeant made him sound like a lavatory attendant and she'd used the voice she kept for grand dowager parts.

"What about him?" he said belligerently.

"When are you going to catch him?" She said it with all the patience of an infant teacher explaining the school rules to a rather backward child on his first day. "After all, there are enough of you."

"I know, Mrs. Beresford," Miller said. "We're pretty hot on parking tickets, but not so good on maniacs who walk the streets on wet nights murdering women."

"There's no need to be rude, Sergeant," she said frostily.

"Oh, but I'm not." Behind him Joanna Hartmann moved in anxiously, Frank Marlowe at her shoulder. Miller leaned down and said, "You see the difficulty about this kind of case is that the murderer could be anyone, Mrs. Beresford. Your own husband—your brother even." He nodded around the room. "Any one of the men here." There was an expression of real alarm on her face, but he didn't let go. "What about Mr. Marlowe, for instance?"

He slipped an edge of authority into his voice and said to Marlowe, "Would you care to account for your movements between the hours of eight and nine last night, sir? I must warn you, of course, that anything you say may be taken down and used in evidence."

Mary Beresford gave a shocked gasp, Marlowe looked decidedly worried and at that precise moment the record on the stereogram came to an end.

Joanna Hartmann grabbed Miller's arm. "Come and play the piano for us." She pulled him away and called brightly over her shoulder to Marlowe who stood there, a drink in each hand, mouth gaping. "He's marvellous. You'd swear it was Oscar Peterson."

Miller was angry, damned angry, but not only at Mary Beresford. She couldn't help being the woman she was, but he was tired of the sort of vicious attack on the police that met him every time he picked up a newspaper, tired of cheap remarks and jibes about police inefficiency from members of the public who didn't seem to appreciate that every detective who could be spared had been working ninety to a hundred hours a week since the Rainlover had first killed, in an attempt to root him out. But how did you find one terrifyingly insane human being in a city of three-quarters of a million? A man with no record, who did not kill for gain, who did not even kill for sexual reasons. Someone who just killed out of some dark compulsion that even the psychiatrists hadn't been able to help them with.

The piano was the best, a Bechstein grand and he sat down, swallowed the double gin and tonic that Marlowe handed him and moved into a cool and complicated version of "The Lady Is a Tramp." One or two people came across to stand at the piano watching, because they knew talent when they heard it and playing a good jazz piano was Miller's greatest love. He moved from one number into another. It was perhaps fifteen minutes later when he heard the door bell chime.

"Probably Jack and Bruno," Joanna said to Marlowe. "I'll get it."

Miller had a clear view of the door as she crossed the room. He looked down at the keyboard again and as he slowed to the end of his number, Mary Beresford gave a shocked gasp.

When Miller turned, a spectacularly fleshy-looking young tart in black plastic mac, mini-skirt and knee-length leather boots stood at the top of the steps beside the maid who had apparently got to the door before Joanna. A couple of men moved into the room behind her. It was pretty obvious which was Bruno Faulkner from what Miller had heard, and it was just as obvious what the man was up to as he helped the girl off with her coat and looked quickly around the room, a look of eager expectancy on his face.

Strangely enough it was the girl Miller felt sorry for. She was pretty enough in her own way and very, very nubile with that touch of raw cynicism common to the sort of young woman who has slept around too often and too early. She tilted her chin in a kind of bravado as she looked about her, but she was going to be hurt, that much was obvious. Quite suddenly Miller knew with complete certainty that he didn't like Bruno Faulkner one little bit. He lit a cigarette and started to play—"Blue Moon."

Of course Joanna Hartmann carried it all off superbly as he knew she would. She walked straight up to Faulkner, kissed him on the cheek and said, "Hello, darling, what kept you?"

"I've been working, Joanna," Faulkner told her. "But I'll tell you about that later. First, I'd like you to meet Grace. I hope you don't mind us bringing her along."

"Of course not." She turned to Grace with her most charming smile. "Hello, my dear."

The girl stared at her open-mouthed. "But you're Joanna Hartmann. I've seen you on the telly." Her voice had dropped into a whisper. "I saw your last film."

"I hope you enjoyed it." Joanna smiled sweetly at Morgan. "Jack, be an angel. Get Grace a drink and introduce her to one or two people. See she enjoys herself."

"Glad to, Joanna." Morgan guided the girl away expertly, sat her in a chair by the piano. "I'll get you a drink. Back in a jiffy."

She sat there looking hopelessly out of place. The attitude of the other guests was what interested Miller most. Some of the women were amused in a rather condescending way, others quite obviously highly indignant at having to breathe the same air. Most of the men on the other hand glanced at her covertly with a sort of lascivious approval. Morgan seemed to be taking his time and she put a hand to her hair nervously and tilted her chin at an ageing white-haired lady who looked her over as if she were a lump of dirt.

Miller liked her for that. She was getting the worst kind of raw deal from people who ought to know better, but seldom did, and she was damned if she was going to let them grind her down. He caught her eye and grinned. "Anything you'd like to hear?"

She crossed to the piano and one or two people who had been standing there moved away. "What about 'St. Louis Blues?' " she said. "I like that."

"My pleasure. What's your name?"

"Grace Packard."

He moved into a solid, pushing arrangement of the great jazz classic that had her snapping her fingers. "That's the greatest," she cried, eyes shining. "Do you do this for a living?"

He shook his head. "Kicks, that's all. I couldn't stand the kind of life the pro musicians lead. One-night stands till the early hours, tour after tour and all at the union rate. No icing on that kind of cake."

"I suppose not. Do you come here often?"

"First time."

"I thought so," she grinned with a sort of gamin charm. "A right bunch of zombies."

Morgan arrived with a drink for her. She put it down on top of the piano and clutched at his arm. "This place is like a morgue. Let's live it up a little."

Morgan didn't seem unwilling and followed her

on to the floor. As Miller came to the end of the number someone turned the stereogram on again, probably out of sheer bloody-mindedness. He wasn't particularly worried, got to his feet and moved to the bar. Joanna Hartmann and Faulkner were standing very close together no more than a yard from him and as he waited for the barman to mix him a large gin and tonic, he couldn't help but overhear their conversation.

"Always the lady, Joanna," Faulkner said. "Doesn't anything ever disturb your poise?"

"Poor Bruno, have I spoiled your little joke? Where did you pick her up, by the way?"

"The public bar of The King's Arms. I'd hoped she might enliven the proceedings. At least I've succeeded in annoying Frank from the look on his face. Thanks be for small mercies."

Joanna shook her head and smiled. "What am I going to do with you?"

"I could make several very pleasant suggestions. Variations on a theme, but all eminently worthwhile."

Before she could reply, Mary Beresford approached and Faulkner louted low. "Madam, all homage."

There was real disgust on her face. "You are really the most disgusting man I know. How dare you bring that dreadful creature here."

"Now there's a deathless line if you like. Presumably from one of those Victorian melodramas you used to star in." She flinched visibly and he turned and looked towards the girl who was dancing with Morgan. "In any case what's so dreadful about a rather luscious young bird enjoying herself. But forgive me. I was forgetting how long it was since you were in that happy state, Aunt Mary." The old woman turned and walked away and Faulkner held up a hand defensively. "I know, I've done it again."

"Couldn't you just ignore her?" Joanna asked.

"Sorry, but she very definitely brings out the worst in me. Have a martini."

As the barman mixed them, Joanna noticed Miller and smiled. "Now here's someone I want you to meet, Bruno. Nick Miller. He's a policeman."

Faulkner turned, examined Miller coolly and sighed. "Dammit all, Joanna, there is a limit you know. I do draw the line at coppers. Where on earth did you find him?"

"Oh, I crawled out of the woodwork," Miller said pleasantly, restraining a sudden impulse to put his right foot squarely between Faulkner's thighs.

Joanna looked worried and something moved in the big man's eyes, but at that moment the door chimes sounded. Miller glanced across, mainly out of curiosity. When the maid opened the door he saw Jack Brady standing in the hall, his battered, Irish face infinitely preferable to any that he had so far met with that evening.

He put down his glass and said to Joanna. "Looks as if I'm wanted."

"Surely not," she said in considerable relief.

Miller grinned and turned to Faulkner. "I'd like to say it's been nice, but then you get used to meeting all sorts in my line of work."

He moved through the crowd rapidly before the big man could reply, took his coat and cap from the maid and gave Brady a push into the hall. "Let's get out of here."

The door closed behind them as he pulled on his trenchcoat. Detective Constable Jack Brady shook his head sadly. "Free booze, too. I should be ashamed to take you away."

"Not from that lot you shouldn't. What's up?"

"Gunner Doyle's on the loose."

Miller paused, a frown of astonishment on his face. "What did you say?"

"They moved him into the Infirmary from Manningham Gaol yesterday with suspected food poisoning. Missed him half an hour ago."

"What's he served—two and a half years?"

"Out of a five stretch."

"The daft bastard. He could have been out in another ten months with remission." Miller sighed and shook his head. "Come on then, Jack, let's see if we can find him."

3

Faulkner ordered his third martini and Joanna said, “Where have you been for the past two days?”

“Working,” he told her. “Damned hard. When were you last at the studio?”

“Wednesday.”

“There were three figures in the group then. Now there are four.”

There was real concern in her voice and she put a hand on his arm. “That’s really too much, Bruno, even for you. You’ll kill yourself.”

“Nonesense. When it’s there, it’s got to come out, Joanna. Nothing else matters. You’re a creative artist yourself. You know what I mean.”

"Even so, when this commission is finished you're taking a long holiday."

Frank Marlowe joined them and she said, "I've just been telling Bruno it's time he took a holiday."

"What an excellent idea. Why not the Bahamas? Six months . . . at least."

"I love you too." Faulkner grinned and turned to Joanna. "Coming with me?"

"I'd love to, but Frank's lined me up for the lead in Mannheim's new play. If there's agreement on terms we go into rehearsal next month."

"But you've only just finished a film." Bruno turned to Marlowe and demanded angrily, "What's wrong with you? Can't you ever see beyond ten per cent of the gross?"

As Marlowe put down his glass, his hand was shaking slightly. "Now look, I've taken just about as much as I intend to take from you."

Joanna got in between them quickly. "You're not being fair, Bruno. Frank is the best agent there is, everyone knows that. If a thing wasn't right for me he'd say so. This is too good a chance to miss and it's time I went back to the stage for a while. I've almost forgotten how to act properly."

The door bell chimed again and the maid admitted another couple. "It's Sam Hagerty and his wife,"

Joanna said. "I'll have to say hello. Try to get on, you two. I'll be back soon."

She moved away through the crowd and Marlowe watched her go, his love showing plainly on his face.

Faulkner smiled gently. "A lovely girl, wouldn't you say?"

Marlowe glared at him in a kind of helpless rage and Faulkner turned to the barman. "Two brandies, please. Better make it a large one for my friend. He isn't feeling too well."

Jack Morgan and Grace Packard were dancing to a slow cool blues. She glanced towards Faulkner who was still at the bar. "He's a funny one, isn't he?"

"Who, Bruno?"

She nodded. "Coming to a do like this in those old clothes. Bringing me. Have you known him long?"

"We were at school together."

"What's he do for a living?"

"He's a sculptor."

"I might have known it was something like that. Is he any good?"

"Some people would tell you he's the best there is."

She nodded soberly. "Maybe that explains him. I

mean when you're the best, you don't need to bother about what other people think, do you?"

"I wouldn't know."

"Mind you, he looks a bit of a wild man to me. Look at the way he handled Harold at the pub."

Morgan shrugged. "He's just full of pleasant little tricks like that. Judo, aikido, karate—you name it, Bruno's got it."

"Can he snap a brick in half with the edge of his hand? I saw a bloke do that once on the telly."

"His favourite party trick."

She pulled away from him abruptly and pushed through the crowd to Faulkner.

"Enjoying yourself?" he demanded.

"It's fabulous. I never thought it would be anything like this."

Faulkner turned to Marlowe who stood at his side drinking morosely. "There you are, Frank. Fairy tales do come true after all."

"Jack says you can smash a brick with the edge of your hand," Grace said.

"Only when I'm on my second bottle."

"I saw it on television once, but I thought they'd faked it."

Faulkner shook his head. "It can be done right

enough. Unfortunately I don't happen to have a brick on me right now."

Marlowe seized his chance. "Come now, Bruno," he said, an edge of malice in his voice. "You mustn't disappoint the little lady. We've heard a lot about your prowess at karate . . . a lot of talk, that is. As I remember a karate expert can snap a plank of wood as easily as a brick. Would this do?"

He indicated a hardwood chopping block on the bar and Faulkner grinned. "You've just made a bad mistake, Frank."

He swept the board clean of fruit, balanced it across a couple of ashtrays and raised his voice theatrically. "Give me room, good people. Give me room."

Those near at hand crowded round and Mary Beresford pushed her way to the front followed by Joanna who looked decidedly uncertain about the whole thing.

"What on earth are you doing, Bruno?"

Faulkner ignored her. "A little bit of hush, please."

He gave a terrible cry and his right hand swung down, splintering the block, scattering several glasses. There was a sudden gasp followed by a general buzz of conversation. Grace cried out in delight and Mary Beresford pushed forward.

"When are you going to start acting your age?" she demanded, her accent slipping at least forty-five years. "Smashing the place up like a stupid teenage lout."

"And why don't you try minding your own business, you silly old cow?"

The rage in his voice, the violence in his eyes reduced the room to silence. Mary Beresford stared at him, her face very white, the visible expression one of unutterable shock.

"How dare you," she whispered.

"Another of those deathless lines of yours."

Marlowe grabbed at his arm. "You can't talk to her like that."

Faulkner lashed out sideways without even looking, catching him in the face. Marlowe staggered back, clutching at the bar, glasses flying in every direction.

In the general uproar which followed, Joanna moved forward angrily. "I think you'd better leave, Bruno."

Strangely, Faulkner seemed to have complete control of himself. "Must I?" He turned to Grace. "Looks as though I'm not wanted. Are you coming or staying?" She hesitated and he shrugged. "Suit yourself."

He pushed his way through the crowd to the door.

As he reached it, Grace arrived breathless. "Changed your mind?" he enquired.

"Maybe I have."

He helped her on with her plastic mac. "How would you like to earn a fiver?"

She looked at him blankly. "What did you say?"

"A fiver . . . just to pose for me for a couple of minutes."

"Well, that's a new name for it."

"Are you on?" he said calmly.

She smiled. "Okay."

"Let's go then."

He opened the door and as Grace Packard went out into the hall, Joanna emerged from the crowd and paused at the bottom of the steps. Faulkner remembered her birthday present and took the leather case from his pocket. "Here, I was forgetting." He threw the case and as she caught it, called, "Happy birthday."

He went out, closing the door and Joanna opened the case and took out the pearls. She stood there looking at them, real pain on her face. For a moment she was obviously on the verge of tears, but then her aunt approached and she forced a brave smile.

"Time to eat, everybody. Shall we go into the

other room?" She led the way, the pearls clutched tightly in her hand.

In Faulkner's studio the fire had died down, but it still gave some sort of illumination and the statues waited there in the half-light, dark and menacing. The key rattled in the lock, the door was flung open and Faulkner bustled in, pushing Grace in front of him.

"Better have a little light on the situation."

He flicked the switch and took off his coat. Grace Packard looked round her approvingly. "This is nice . . . and your own bar, too."

She crossed to the bar, took off her mac and gloves, then moved towards the statues. "Is this what you're working on at the moment?"

"Do you like it?"

"I'm not sure." She seemed a trifle bewildered. "They make me feel funny. I mean to say, they don't even look human."

Faulkner chuckled. "That's the general idea." He nodded towards an old Victorian print screen which stood to one side of the statues. "You can undress behind that."

She stared at him blankly. "Undress?"

"But of course," he said. "You're not much use to

me with your clothes on. Now hurry up, there's a good girl. When you're ready, get up on the dais beside the others."

"The others?"

"Beside the statues. I'm thinking of adding another. You can help me decide."

She stood looking at him, hands on hips, her face quite different, cynical and knowing. "What some people will do for kicks."

She disappeared behind the screen and Faulkner poured himself a drink at the bar and switched on the hi-fi to a pleasant, big-band version of "A Nightingale Sang in Berkeley Square." He walked to the fire, humming the tune, got down on one knee and started to add lumps of coal to the flames from a brass scuttle.

"Will this do?" Grace Packard said.

He turned, still on one knee. She had a fine body, firm and sensual, breasts pointed with desire, hands flat against her thighs.

"Well?" she said softly.

Faulkner stood up, still holding his drink, switched off the hi-fi, then moved to the bedroom door and turned off the light. The shapes stood out clearly in silhouette against the great window and Grace Packard merged with the whole, became like the rest of them, a dark shadow that had existence and form, but nothing more.

Faulkner's face in the firelight was quite expressionless. He switched on the light again. "Okay . . . fine. You can get dressed."

"Is that all?" she demanded in astonishment.

"I've seen what I wanted to see if that's what you mean."

"How kinky can you get."

She shook her head in disgust, vanished behind the screen and started to dress again. Faulkner put more coal on the fire. When he had finished, he returned to the bar to freshen his drink. She joined him a moment later carrying her boots.

"That was quick," he told her.

She sat on one of the bar stools and started to pull on her boots. "Not much to take off with this year's fashions. I can't get over it. You really did want me to pose."

"If I'd wanted the other thing I'd have included it in our arrangement." He took a ten-pound note from his wallet and stuffed it down the neck of her dress. "I promised you a fiver. There's ten for luck."

"You *must* be crazy." She examined the note quickly, then lifted her skirt and slipped it into the top of her right stocking.

He was amused and showed it. "Your personal bank?"

"As good as. You know, I can't make you out."

"The secret of my irresistible attraction."

"Is that a fact?"

He helped her on with her mac. "Now I've got some work to do."

She grabbed for her handbag as he propelled her towards the door. "Heh, what is this? Don't say it's the end of a beautiful friendship."

"Something like that. Now be a good girl and run along home. There's a taxi rank just round the corner."

"That's all right. I haven't far to go." She turned as he opened the door and smiled impishly. "Sure you want me to leave?"

"Goodnight, Grace," Faulkner said firmly.

He closed the door, turned and moved slowly to the centre of the room. There was a dull ache just to one side of the crown of his skull and as he touched the spot briefly, feeling the indentation of the scar, a slight nervous tic developed in the right cheek. He stood there examining the statues for a moment, then went to the cigarette box on the coffee table. It was empty. He cursed softly and quickly searched his pockets without success.

A search behind the bar proved equally fruitless

and he pulled on his raincoat and hat quickly. As he passed the bar, he noticed a pair of gloves on the floor beside one of the stools and picked them up. The girl had obviously dropped them in the final hurried departure. Still, with any luck he would catch up with her before she reached the square. He stuffed them into his pocket and went out quickly.

Beyond, through the great window, the wind moaned in the night, driving the rain across the city in a dark curtain.

4

When they carried Sean Doyle into the General Infirmary escape couldn't have been further from his mind. He was sweating buckets, had a temperature of 104 and his stomach seemed to bulge with pieces of broken glass that ground themselves into his flesh and organs ferociously.

He surfaced twenty-four hours later, weak and curiously light-headed, but free from pain. The room was in half-darkness, the only light a small lamp which stood on the bedside locker. One of the screws from the prison, an ex-Welsh Guardsman called Jones, nodded on a chair against the wall as per regulations.

Doyle moistened cracked lips and tried to whistle, but at that moment the door opened and a staff nurse entered, a towel over her arm. She was West Indian, dark and supple. To Doyle after two and a half years on the wrong side of the wall, the Queen of Sheba herself couldn't have looked more desirable.

As she moved across to the bed, he closed his eyes quickly. He was aware of her closeness, warm and perfumed with lilac, the rustle of her skirt as she turned and tip-toed across to Jones. Doyle watched her from beneath lowered eyelids as the Welshman came awake with a start.

"Here, what's going on?" he said in some alarm. "Is the Gunner all right?"

She put out a hand to restrain him. "He's still asleep. Would you like to go down to the canteen?"

"Well, I shouldn't really you know," Jones told her in his high Welsh voice.

"You'll be all right, I'll stay," she said. "Nothing can possibly happen—he's still asleep. After what he's been through he must be as weak as a kitten."

"All right then," Jones whispered. "A cup of tea and a smoke. I'll be back in ten minutes."

As they moved to the door she said, "Tell me, why do you call him the Gunner?"

Jones chuckled. "Well, that's what he was you see.

A gunner in the Royal Artillery. Then when he came out and went into the ring, that's what they called him. Gunner Doyle."

"He was a prizefighter?"

"One of the best middleweights in the game." Jones was unable to keep the enthusiasm from his voice for like most Welshmen he was a fanatic where boxing was concerned. "North of England champion. Might have been a contender if he could have left the skirts alone."

"What was his crime?" she whispered, curiosity in her voice.

"Now there he did really manage to scale the heights as you might say." Jones chuckled at his own wit. "He was a cat burglar—one of the best in the game and it's a dying art, believe me. Climb anything he could."

The door closed behind him and the staff nurse turned and looked across at the Gunner. He lowered his eyelids softly as she came across to the bed. He was acutely aware of her closeness, the perfume filled his nostrils, lilac, heavy and clinging, fresh after rain, his favourite flower. The stiff uniform dress rustled as she leaned across him to put the towel on the table on the other side.

The Gunner opened his eyes and took in everything. The softly rounded curves, the dress riding up her thighs as she leaned across, the black stockings shining in the lamplight. With a sudden fierce chuckle he cupped his right hand around her left leg and slid it up inside her skirt to the band of warm flesh at the top of her stocking.

"By God, that's grand," he said.

Her eyes were very round as she turned to look at him. For a frozen moment she stared into his face, then jumped backwards with a little cry. She stared at him in astonishment and the Gunner grinned.

"I once shared a cell at the Ville with a bloke who did that to a big blonde who was standing in front of him in a bus queue one day. Just for a laugh. They gave him a year in the nick. Makes you wonder what the country's coming to."

She turned without a word and rushed out, the door bouncing back against the wall before closing. It occurred to the Gunner almost at once that she wasn't coming back. Add that to the fact that Jones would be at least fifteen minutes in the canteen and it left a situation that was full of possibilities.

It also occurred to him that with full remission he had only another ten months of his sentence to serve, but at that sudden exciting moment, ten months stretched into an infinity that had no end. He flung the bedclothes to one side and swung his legs to the floor.

An athlete by profession all his life, the Gunner had taken good care to keep himself in first-class physical trim even in prison and this probably accounted for the fact that apart from a moment of giddiness as he first stood up, he felt no ill effects at all as he crossed to the locker against the wall and opened it. There was an old dressing-gown inside, but no slippers. He pulled it on quickly, opened the door and peered out into the corridor.

It was anything but deserted. Two doctors stood no more than ten yards away deep in conversation and a couple of porters pushed a floor polisher between them, its noiseless hum vibrating on the air. The Gunner turned and walked the other way without hesitation. When he turned the corner at the far end he found himself in a cul-de-sac. There was a service elevator facing him and a door at the side of it opened on to a dark concrete stairway. The elevator was on its way up so he took the stairs, running down lightly, the concrete cold on his bare feet.

Ten floors down, he arrived at the basement, opened the door at the bottom and found himself in a small entrance hall. One door opened into a side courtyard, heavy rain slanting down through the lamp that was bracketed to the wall above the entrance. But he wouldn't last five minutes out there on a night like this without shoes and some decent clothes. He turned and opened the other door and immediately heard voices approaching. Without hesitation he plunged into the heavy rain, crossed the tiny courtyard and turned into the street keeping close to the wall.

"So you were only out of the room for fifteen minutes?" Brady said.

"As long as it took me to get down to the canteen, have a cup of tea and get back again." Jones' face was white and drawn. "The dirty bastard. Why did he have to do this to me? God knows what might happen. I could lose my pension."

"You've only yourself to blame," Miller said coldly. "So don't start trying to put it on to Doyle. He saw his chance and took it. Nobody can blame him for that."

He dismissed the prison officer with a nod and turned to the young staff nurse. "You told Jones you'd stay in the room till he got back. Why did you leave?"

She struggled with the truth for a moment, but the

thought of recounting in detail what had happened to the two police officers was more than she could bear.

"I'd things to do," she said. "I thought it would be all right. He was asleep."

"Or so it seemed. I understand you told the first officer you saw that there was only an old dressing-gown in the cupboard?"

"That's right."

"But no shoes or slippers?"

"Definitely not."

Miller nodded and went out into the corridor, Brady at his heels. "All right, Jack, you're Doyle in a hurry in bare feet and a dressing-gown. What do you do?"

Brady glanced left along the quiet end of the corridor and led the way. He paused at the lift, frowned, then opened the door and peered down into the dark well of the concrete stairway.

"On a hunch I'd say he went this way. A lot safer than the lift."

They went down quickly and at the bottom Miller pushed open the outside door and looked out into the rain. "Not very likely. He'd need clothes."

The other door led into a narrow corridor lined on one side with half a dozen green painted lockers. Each one was padlocked and carried an individual's name on a small white card. They were aware of the gentle hum of the oil-fired heating plant somewhere near at hand and in a small office at the end of the corridor, they found the chief technician.

Miller showed him his warrant card. "Looking for the bloke that skipped out are you?" the man said.

"That's right. He'd need clothes. Anything missing down here?"

"Not a chance," the chief technician shook his head. "I don't know if you noticed, but all the lads keep their lockers padlocked. That was on advice from one of your blokes after we had a lot of pinching last year. Too easy for people to get in through the side door."

Miller thanked him and they went back along the corridor, and stood on the steps looking out at the driving rain.

"You're thinking he just walked out as he was?" Brady suggested.

Miller shrugged. "He didn't have much time remember. One thing's certain—he couldn't afford to hang about."

Brady shook his head. "He wouldn't last long in his bare feet on a night like this. Bound to be spotted by someone sooner or later."

"As I see it he has three possible choices," Miller

said. "He can try to steal a car, but that's messy because he's got to nose his way round till he finds one that some idiot's forgotten to lock and in that rig-out of his, he's certain to be noticed."

"He could always hang around some alley and wait his chance to mug the first bloke who went by."

Miller nodded. "My second choice, but it's still messy and there aren't many people around the back streets on a night like this. He could get pneumonia waiting. My own hunch is that he's making for somewhere definite. Somewhere not too far away perhaps. Who were his friends?"

"Come off it, he didn't have any." Brady chuckled. "Except for the female variety. The original sexual athlete, the Gunner. Never happy unless he had three or four birds on the go at once."

"What about Mona Freeman?" Miller said. "He was going to marry her."

"She was a mug if she believed him." Brady shook his head. "She's still in Holloway. Conspiracy to defraud last year."

"All right then," Miller said. "Get out the street directory and let's take a look at the map. Something might click while you're looking at it."

Brady had grown old on the streets of the city and had developed an extraordinary memory for places and faces, the minutiae of city life. Now he unfolded the map at the back of his pocket directory and examined the area around the infirmary. He gave a sudden grunt. "Doreen Monaghan."

"I remember her," Miller said. "Little Irish girl of seventeen just over from the bogs. She thought the sun shone out of the Gunner's backside."

"Well, she isn't seventeen any longer," Brady said. "Has a flat in a house in Jubilee Terrace less than a quarter of a mile from here. Been on the game just over a year now."

"Let's go then." Miller grinned. "And don't forget that right of his whatever happens. He's only got to connect once and you won't wake up till next Friday."

5

When the Gunner hurried across the courtyard and turned into the side street at the rear of the infirmary, he hadn't the slightest idea what he was going to do next. Certainly he had no particular destination in mind although the icy coldness of the wet flags beneath his bare feet told him that he'd better find one quickly.

The rain was hammering down now which at least kept the streets clear and he paused on a corner to consider his next move. The sign abovc his head read Jubilee Street and triggered off a memory process that finally brought him to Doreen Monaghan who at one time had worshipped the ground he walked on. She'd written regularly during the first six months of his sentence when he was at Pentonville, but then the letters had tailed off and gradually faded away. The important thing was that she lived at 15, Jubilee Terrace and might still be there.

He kept to the back streets to avoid company and arrived at his destination ten minutes later, a tall, decaying Victorian town house in a twilight area where a flat was high living and most families managed on one room.

The fence had long since disappeared and the garden was a wilderness of weeds and brambles, the privet hedge so tall that the weight of the heavy rain bowed it over. He paused for a moment and looked up. Doreen had had the top floor flat stretching from the front of the house to the rear and light showed dimly through a gap in the curtains which was encouraging.

When he went into the porch there was an innovation, a row of independent letter boxes for mail, each one neatly labelled. Doreen's name was there all right underneath the one at the end and he grinned as he went in through the hall and mounted the stairs. She was certainly in for one hell of a surprise.

The lady in question was at that moment in bed with an able seaman of Her Majesty's Royal Navy home on leave from the Far East and already regretting the dark-skinned girls of Penang and Singapore who knew what it was for and didn't charge too much.

A member of the oldest profession in the world, she had long since discovered that its rewards far exceeded anything that shop or factory could offer and salved her conscience with a visit to the neighbouring church of Christ the King every Monday for confession followed by Mass.

Her sailor having drifted into the sleep of exhaustion, she gently eased herself from beneath the sheets, pulled on an old kimono and lit a cigarette. Having undressed in something of a hurry, his uniform lay on the floor beside a chair and as she picked it up, a leather wallet fell to the floor. There must have been eighty or ninety pounds in there—probably his leave money. She extracted a couple of fivers, slipped them under the edge of the mat, then replaced the wallet.

He stirred and she moved across to the dressing-table and started to put on her stockings. He pushed himself up on one elbow and said sleepily, "Going out, then?"

"Three quid doesn't get you squatter's rights you know," she said. "Come on now, let's have you out of there and dressed. The night isn't half over and I've things to do."

At that moment there was a knock at the door. She straightened, surprise on her face. The knocking continued, low but insistent.

She moved to the door and said softly, "Yes?"

The voice that replied was muffled beyond all recognition. "Come on, Doreen, open up," it called. "See what Santa's brought you."

"Who is it?" the sailor called, an edge of alarm in his voice.

Doreen ignored him, opened the door on its chain and peered out. Sean Doyle stood there in a pool of water, soaked to the skin, hair plastered to his skull, the scarlet hospital dressing-gown clinging to his lean body like a second skin.

He grinned, the old wicked grin that used to put her on her back in five seconds flat. "Come on then, darling, I'm freezing to death out here."

So complete was the surprise, so great the shock of seeing him that she unhooked the chain in a kind of dazed wonder and backed slowly into the room. As the Gunner moved in after her and closed the door the sailor skipped out of bed and pulled on his underpants.

"Here, what's the bloody game?" he demanded.

The Gunner ignored him, concentrating completely on Doreen whose ample charms were prominently displayed for the girdle of her kimono, loosely fastened, had come undone.

"By God, but you're a sight for sore eyes," he said, sincere admiration in his voice.

Having had time to take in the Gunner's bedraggled appearance, the sailor's alarm had subsided and there was an edge of belligerency in his voice when he spoke again, "I don't know who the hell you are, mate, but you'll bloody well get out of it fast if you know what's good for you."

The Gunner looked him over and grinned amiably. "Why don't you shut up, sonny?"

The sailor was young, active and muscular and fancied himself as a fighting man. He came round the end of the bed with a rush, intending to throw this rash intruder out on his ear and made the biggest mistake of his life. The Gunner's left foot slipped forward, knee turned slightly in. The sailor flung the sort of punch that he had seen used frequently and with great success on the films. The Gunner swayed a couple of inches and the punch slid across his shoulder. His left fist screwed into the sailor's solar plexus, his right connected with the edge of the jaw, slamming him back against the far wall from which he rebounded to fall on his face unconscious.

The Gunner turned, untying the cord of his

dressing-gown. "How've you been keeping them, darlin?' he demanded cheerfully.

"But Gunner—what happened?" she said.

"They had me in the infirmary for a check-up. One of the screws got a bit dozy so I took my chance and hopped it. Got any clothes?"

She opened a drawer, took out a clean towel and gave it to him, an expression of wonder still on her face. "No—nothing that would do for you."

"Never mind—I'll take this bloke's uniform." He turned her round and slapped her backside. "Find me something to drink, there's a girl. It was no joke out there in this rig-out on a night like this."

She went into the kitchen and he could hear her opening cupboards as he stripped and scrubbed himself dry. He had the sailor's trousers and shirt on and was trying to squeeze his feet into the shoes when she returned.

He tossed them into the corner in disgust. "No bloody good. Two sizes too small. What have you got there?"

"Sherry," she said. "It's all I could find. I was never much of a drinker—remember?"

The bottle was about half-full and he uncorked it and took a long swallow. He wiped a hand across his mouth with a sigh of pleasure as the wine burned its way into his stomach.

"Yes, I remember all right." He emptied the bottle and dropped it on the floor. "I remember lots of things."

He opened her kimono gently, and his sigh seemed to echo into forever. Still sitting on the edge of the bed, he pulled her close to him, burying his face in her breasts.

She ran her fingers through his hair and said urgently, "Look, Gunner, you've got to get moving."

"There's always time for this," he said and looked up at her, his eyes full of grey smoke. "All the time in the world."

He fell back across the bed, pulling her down on top of him and there was a knock on the door.

Doreen jumped up, pulling her kimono about her and demanded loudly. "Who is it?"

The voice that replied was high and clear. "Mrs. Goldberg, dear. I'd like a word with you."

"My landlady," Doreen whispered and raised her voice. "Can't it wait?"

"I'm afraid not, dear. It really is most urgent."

"What am I going to do?" Doreen demanded desperately. "She's a funny old bird. She could make a lot of trouble for me."

"Does she know you're on the game?" the Gunner demanded.

"At fifteen quid a week for this rat-trap? What do you think?"

"Fair enough." The Gunner rolled the unconscious sailor under the bed, lay on it quickly, head propped up against a pillow and helped himself to a cigarette from a packet on the bedside locker. "Go on, let her in now. I'm just another client."

Mrs. Goldberg called out again impatiently and started to knock as Doreen crossed to the door and opened it on the chain. The Gunner heard the old woman say, "I must see you, my dear. It's very, very urgent."

Doreen shrugged and unfastened the chain. She gave a cry of dismay as the door was pushed back sending her staggering across the room to sprawl across the Gunner on the bed.

Nick Miller moved in, Brady at his side, the local patrolman behind them, resplendent in black crash helmet and foul-weather gear.

"All right then, Gunner," Miller said cheerfully. "Let's be having you."

The Gunner laughed out loud. "Another five minutes and I'd have come quietly, Mr. Miller, but to hell with this for a game of soldiers."

He gave the unfortunate Doreen a sudden, violent push that sent her staggering into Miller's arms, sprang from the bed and was into the kitchen before anyone could make a move. The door slammed in Brady's face as he reached it and the bolt clicked home. He turned and nodded to the young patrolman, a professional rugby player with the local team, who tucked his head into his shoulder and charged as if he was carving his way through a pack of Welsh forwards.

In the kitchen, the Gunner tugged ineffectually at the window, then grabbed a chair and smashed an exit. A second later, the door caved in behind him as the patrolman blasted through and sprawled on his face.

There was a fallpipe about five feet to one side. Without hesitation, the Gunner reached for the rotting gutter above his head, swung out into the rain and grabbed at the pipe as the gutter sagged and gave way.

He hung there for a moment, turned and grinned at Miller who leaned out of the window, arm outstretched and three feet too short.

"No hard feelings, Mr. Miller. See you in church."

He went down the pipe like a monkey and disappeared into the darkness and rain below. Miller turned and grinned at Brady. "Still in his bare feet, did you notice? He always was good for a laugh."

They returned to the bedroom to find Doreen

weeping passionately. She flung herself into Brady's arms the moment he appeared. "Oh, help me, Mr. Brady. As God's my judge I didn't know that divil was coming here this night."

Her accent had thickened appreciably and Brady patted her bottom and shoved her away. "You needn't put that professional Irish act on with me, Doreen Monaghan. It won't work. I'm a Cork man meself."

There was a muffled groan from under the bed. Brady leaned down and grabbed a foot, hauling the sailor into plain view, naked except for his underpants.

"Now I'd say that just about rounds the night off," Miller said to the big Irishman and they both started to laugh.

Mrs. Goldberg, seventy and looking every year of it with her long jet earrings and a patina of make-up that gave her a distinct resemblance to a death mask, peered round the door and viewed the splintered door with horror.

"Oh, my God," she said. "The damage. Who's going to pay for the damage?"

The young patrolman appeared behind her, looking white and shaken. Miller moved forward, ignoring Mrs. Goldberg for the moment. "What happened to you?"

"Thought I'd better get a general call out for Doyle as soon as possible, Sergeant, so I went straight down to my bike."

"Good lad," Brady said. "That's using your nut."

"They've been trying to get in touch with Sergeant Miller for the last ten minutes or so."

"Oh, yes," Miller said. "Anything important?"

"Chief Superintendent Mallory wants you to meet him at Dob Court, Sergeant. That's off Gascoigne Street on the north side of Jubilee Park. The beat man found a woman there about twenty minutes ago." Suddenly he looked sick. "Looks like another Rainlover killing."

There were at least a dozen patrol cars in Gascoigne Street when Miller and Brady arrived in the Mini-Cooper and the Studio, the Forensic Department's travelling laboratory, was just drawing up as they got out and moved along the wet pavement to Dob Court.

As they approached, two men emerged and stood talking. One was Detective Inspector Henry Wade, Head of Forensic, a fat balding man who wore horn-rimmed spectacles and a heavy overcoat. He usually smiled a lot, but now he looked grim and serious as he wiped rain from his glasses with a handkerchief and listened to what Detective Chief Superintendent George Mallory of Scotland Yard's Murder Squad was saying to him.

He nodded and moved away and Mallory turned to Miller. "Where were you?"

He was forty-five years of age, crisp, intelligent, the complete professional. The provincials he had to work with usually didn't like him, which suited him down to the ground because he detested inefficiency in any form and had come across too much of it for comfort on his forays outside London.

He thoroughly approved of Miller with his sharp intelligence and his law degree, because it was in such men that the salvation of the country's outdated police system lay. Under no circumstances would he have dreamt of making his approval apparent.

"Brady and I had a lead on Doyle."

"The prisoner who escaped from the infirmary? What happened?"

Miller told him briefly and Mallory nodded. "Never mind that now. Come and have a look at this."

The body lay a little way inside the alley covered with a coat against the heavy rain until the Studio boys could get a tarpaulin rigged. The constable who stood beside it held his torch close as Mallory lifted the raincoat.

"From the looks of it her neck is broken just like the others," Mallory said, "but the first thing we've got to do is find out who she is. Typical of a lot of these girls these days there isn't any kind of identification whatsoever in her handbag."

Miller looked down at the waxen face turned sideways awkwardly, the eyes staring into eternity. When he spoke, it was with difficulty.

"I think I can help you there, sir."

"You know her?"

"Her name is Packard, sir," Miller said hoarsely. "Grace Packard."

6

The Gunner went through the back gate of the yard at the rear of Doreen's house and ran like a hare, turning from one street into another without hesitation, completely forgetting his bare feet in the excitement of the moment.

When he paused in a doorway for a breather, his heart was pounding like a trip-hammer, but not because he was afraid. On the contrary, he found himself in the grip of a strange exhilaration. A psychologist might have found a reason in the sudden release from confinement after two and a half years in a prison cell. The Gunner only knew that he was free and he lifted his face up to the rain and laughed out loud. The chase was on. He would lose it in the end, he knew that, but he'd give them a run for their money.

He moved towards the end of the street and paused. A woman's voice said clearly, "Able-fox-victor come in please. I have a 952 for you."

He peered round the corner and saw a police car parked, window open as a beat constable in helmet and cape leaned down to speak to the driver. The Gunner retreated hastily and trotted towards the far end of the street. He was no more than half-way along when a police motor cyclist turned the corner and came towards him. The man saw him at once and came on with a sudden burst of speed, engine roaring. The Gunner ran across the street and ducked into a narrow entry between two houses.

He found himself in a small courtyard faced by a stone wall a good fifteen feet high and in one corner was an old wash-house of the type common to late Victorian houses. He pulled himself up on to the sloping roof as the patrolman pounded into the entry blowing his whistle, and reached for the top of the wall, sliding over silently as the policeman arrived.

The sound of the whistle faded as he worked his way through a network of backyards and alleys that stretched towards the south side of Jubilee Park. He stopped once as a police car's siren sounded close by and then another lifted on the night air in the middle distance. He started to run again. The bastards were certainly doing him proud.

Ten minutes later he had almost reached the park when another siren not too far in front of him made him pause. It was standard police procedure on this sort of chase, he knew that, intended to confuse and bewilder the quarry until he did something stupid.

But the Gunner was too old a fox for that one. The park was out. What he needed now was somewhere to lie up for a few hours until the original excitement had died down.

He retraced his steps and turned into the first side street. It was flanked by high walls and on the left, a massive wooden gate carried the sign *Henry Crowther and Sons—Transport*. It seemed just the sort of place he was looking for and for once his luck was in. There was the usual small judas with a yale lock set in the main gate. Someone had left it on the latch for it opened to his touch.

He found four trucks parked close together in a cobbled yard. There was a house at the other end and light streamed between the curtains of a ground floor window.

When he peered inside he saw a white-haired old

woman sitting in front of a bright coal fire watching television. She had a cigarette in one hand and what looked like a glass of whisky in the other. He envied her both and was conscious of his feet for the first time since leaving Doreen's flat. They were cold and raw and hurt like hell. He hobbled across the yard towards a building on the right of the house and went in through doors which stood open. It had been a stable in years gone by, but from the looks of things was now used as a workshop or garage.

Wooden stairs went up through a board floor to what had obviously been the hayloft. It was in almost total darkness and seemed to be full of drums of oil and assorted junk. A half-open wooden door creaked uneasily and rain drifted in on the wind. A small wooden platform jutted out ten feet above the cobbles and a block and tackle hung from a loading hook.

He had a good view of the house and the yard, which was important, and sank down on an old tarpaulin and started to massage his feet vigorously. They hadn't felt like this since Korea and he shuddered as old memories of frostbite and comrades who had lost toes and even feet in that terrible retreat south during the first winter campaign came back to him.

The gate clicked in the darkness below and he straightened and peered out. Someone hurried across the yard and opened the front door. As light streamed out, he saw that it was a young woman in a raincoat with a scarf bound around her head, peasant-fashion. She looked pretty wet and the Gunner smiled as she went inside and closed the door.

He leaned against the wall and stared into the rain, hunger gnawing at his stomach. Not that there was anything he could do about that. Later, perhaps, when all the lights had gone out in the house he might see if he had lost any of his old skill. Shoes and something to eat and maybe an old raincoat—that's all he needed. If he could make it as far as the Ring Road there were any one of half a dozen transport cafés where long-distance lorry drivers pulled up for rest and a meal. All he had to do was get himself into the back of a truck and he could be two hundred miles away by breakfast.

He flinched, dazzled by light that poured from one of the second floor windows. When he looked across he could see the girl standing in the doorway of what was obviously her bedroom. The wind lifted, driving rain before it and the judas gate creaked. The Gunner peered cautiously into the darkness, imagining for a moment that someone else had arrived, then turned his attention to the bedroom again.

The girl didn't bother to draw the curtains, secure

in the knowledge that she was cut off from the street by the high wall and started to undress, obviously soaked to the skin.

The Gunner watched with frank and open admiration. Two and a half years in the nick and the only female company a monthly visit from his Aunty Mary, a seventy-year-old Irish woman with a heart of corn whose visits with their acid asides on authority, the peelers as she still insisted on calling them, and life in general, always kept him laughing for at least a week afterwards. But this? Now this was different.

The young woman dried off with a large white towel, then examined herself critically in the mirror. Strange how few women looked their best in the altogether, but she was more than passable. The black hair almost reached the pointed breasts and a narrow waist swelled into hips that were perhaps a trifle too large for some tastes, but suited the Gunner down to the ground.

When she dressed again, she didn't bother with a suspender belt. Simply pulled on a pair of hold-up stockings, black pants and bra, then took a dress from the wardrobe. He'd heard they were wearing them short since he'd gone down, but this was ridiculous. Not only was it half-way up her thighs, but crocheted into the bargain so you could see through it like the tablecloth Aunty Mary had kept in the parlour when he was a kid.

She stood at the dressing table and started to brush her hair, perhaps the most womanly of all actions, and the Gunner felt strangely sad. He'd started off by fancying a bit of the usual and why not? He'd almost forgotten what it tasted like and the business with Doreen had certainly put him in the mood. But now, lying there in the loft with the rain falling, he felt like some snotty-nosed kid with his arse out of his pants, looking in at what he could never have and no one to blame but himself.

She tied her hair back with a velvet ribbon, crossed to the door and went out, switching off the light. The Gunner sighed and eased back slightly and below in the yard there was the scrape of a foot on stone.

Jenny Crowther was twenty-two years of age, a practical, hard-headed Yorkshire girl who had never visited London in her life, but in her crocheted minidress and dark stockings she would have passed in the West End without comment.

"Feeling better, love?" her grandmother enquired as she entered the room.

Jenny nodded, rubbing her hands as she approached the fire. "It's nice to be dry."

"Eh, Jenny love," the old woman said. "I don't know how you can wear yon dress. I can see your knickers."

"You're supposed to, Gran." The old woman stared in blank amazement across a gulf that was exactly fifty years wide and the girl picked up the empty coal scuttle. "I'll get some coal, then we'll have a nice cup of tea."

The coal was in a concrete bunker to the left of the front door and when she opened it, light flooded across the yard, outlining her thighs clearly through the crocheted dress as she paused, looking at the rain. She took an old raincoat from a peg, hitched it over her shoulders, went down the steps and lifted the iron trap at the base of the coal bunker. There was no sound and yet she turned, aware from some strange sixth sense of the danger that threatened her. She caught a brief glimpse of a dark shape, the vague blur of a face beneath a rain hat, and then great hands had her by the throat.

* * *

The Gunner went over the edge of the platform, hung for a moment at the end of the block and tackle, then dropped to the cobbles. He moved in fast, smashing a fist into the general area of the other man's kidneys when he got close enough. It was like hitting a rock wall. The man flung the girl away from him and turned. For a moment, the Gunner saw the face clearly, lips drawn back in a snarl. An arm swept sideways with amazing speed, bunched knuckles catching him on the side of the head, sending him back against one of the trucks. The Gunner went down on one knee and the girl's attacker went past him in a rush. The judas banged and the man's running steps faded along the back street.

As the Gunner got to his feet, Ma Crowther called from the doorway, "Make another move and I'll blow your head off."

She was holding a double-barrelled shotgun, the barrels of which had been sawn down to nine inches in length, transforming it into one of the most dangerous and vicious weapons in the book.

Jenny Crowther moved away from the wall, a hand to her throat and shook her head. "Not him, Gran. I don't know where he came from, but it was a good job he was around."

The Gunner was impressed. Any other bird he'd

ever known, even the really hard knocks, would have been on their backs after an experience like that, but not this one.

"Which mob were you in then, the Guards?" he demanded.

The girl turned to look at him, grinning instantly and something was between them at once, unseen perhaps, but almost physical in its strength. Like meeting like, with instantaneous recognition.

She looked him over, taking in the sailor's uniform, the bare feet and laughed, a hand to her mouth. "Where on earth did you spring from?"

"The loft," the Gunner told her.

"Shall I get the police, love?" Ma Crowther asked.

The Gunner cut in quickly. "Why bother the peelers about a little thing like this? You know what it's like on a Saturday night. A bloke has a few pints, then follows the first bit of skirt he sees. Sometimes he tries to go a bit too far like the geezer who just skipped, but it's all come out in the wash. Once it's reported in the papers, all the old dears will think he screwed you, darlin', even if he didn't," he assured the girl gaily.

"Here, just a minute," the old woman said. "Bare feet and dressed like a sailor. I know who you are." She turned to the girl and said excitedly, "They've just had a flash on Northern Newscast. This is Gunner Doyle."

"Gunner Doyle?" the girl said.

"The boxer. Your Dad used to take me to see him. Topped the bill at the Town Hall a couple of times. Doing five years at Manningham Gaol. They took him into the infirmary because they thought he was ill and he gave them the slip earlier this evening."

The girl stood looking at him, legs slightly apart, a hand on her hip and the Gunner managed a tired, tired grin. "That's me, the original naughty boy."

"I don't know about that," she said. "But you're bleeding like a stuck pig. Better come inside." She turned and took the shotgun from the old woman's grasp. "It's all right, Gran. He won't bite."

"You forgot something," the Gunner said.

She turned in the doorway. "What's that, then?"

"What you came out for in the first place." He picked up the coal scuttle. "Lad's work, that's what my Aunty Mary always used to say."

He got down on his knees to fill it. When he straightened and turned wearily, the girl said, "I don't know why, but I think I like your Aunty Mary."

The Gunner grinned. "She'd go for you, darlin'. I'll tell you that for nothing."

He swayed suddenly and she reached out and caught his arm in a grip of surprising strength. "Come on then, soldier, you've had enough for one night," and she drew him into the warmth.

7

Faulkner frowned, enormous concentration on his face as he leaned over the drawing board and carefully sketched in another line. When the door bell rang he ignored it and continued working. There was another more insistent ring. He cursed softly, covered the sketch with a clean sheet of cartridge paper and went to the door.

He opened it to find Chief Superintendent Mallory standing there, Miller at his shoulder. Mallory smiled politely. "Mr. Faulkner? Chief Superintendent Mallory. I believe you've already met Detective Sergeant Miller."

Faulkner showed no particular surprise, but his eyes widened slightly when he looked at Miller. "What is all this? Tickets for the policeman's ball?"

Mallory's manner was dangerously gentle. "I wonder if we could have a few words with you, sir?"

Faulkner stood to one side, ushering them into the studio with a mock bow. "Be my guest, Superintendent."

He closed the door and as he turned to face them, Mallory said in a calm, matter-of-fact voice, "We're making enquiries concerning a Miss Packard, Mr. Faulkner. I understand you might be able to help us?"

Faulkner lit a cigarette and shrugged. "To the best of my knowledge I've never even heard of her."

"But she was with you earlier this evening at Joanna Hartmann's party," Miller put in.

"Oh, you mean Grace?" Faulkner nodded. "I'm with you now. So the viper's discovered it can sting, has it? Has he made a formal complaint?"

"I'm afraid I don't understand you, sir," Mallory said. "Grace Packard is dead. Her body was found in an alley called Dob Court not far from here less than an hour ago. Her neck was broken."

There was a short silence during which both policemen watched Faulkner closely, waiting for some reaction. He seemed genuinely bewildered and put a hand to his forehead. "Either of you feel like a drink?"

Mallory shook his head. "No thank you, sir."

"Well, I do." He moved to the fire and tossed his cigarette into the flames. "You say she was found about an hour ago?"

"That's right." Faulkner glanced up at the clock. It was just coming on to eleven-thirty-five and Mallory said, "What time did she leave here?"

Faulkner turned slowly. "Who said she was here at all?" He looked at Miller with a frown. "Have you been bothering Joanna?"

Miller shook his head. "When I telephoned, the party was still going strong from the sound of things. I spoke to the maid. She told me that you and the girl had left together."

"All right—she was here, but for no more than ten minutes. I left at half-ten."

"Which would indicate that she was murdered almost immediately," Mallory said.

"Is this another of those Rainlover things?"

"We can't be sure yet. Let's say it falls into a familiar pattern."

"Two in two days." Faulkner was by now quite obviously over the initial shock. "He's getting out of hand."

Miller watched his every move, slightly puzzled. The man actually seemed to be enjoying the whole sorry business. He wondered what Faulkner had in his veins instead of blood and the big man said, "I hope you won't mind me asking, but am I first on the list?"

"This is an informal interview, sir, solely to help us in our enquiries," Mallory told him. "Of course you're perfectly entitled to have your solicitor present."

"Wouldn't dream of dragging him away from the party," Faulkner said. "He deserves it. You just fire away. I'll do anything I can to help."

"You made a rather puzzling remark when we first came in," Miller said. "Something about a viper discovering that it could sting. What did you mean by that?"

"I might as well tell you, I suppose. I've been working rather hard lately and completely forgot about Joanna's birthday party. A friend, Mr. Jack Morgan, called for me and we stopped in at The King's Arms in Lazer Street for a quick one. While we were there, the girl came in."

"And you got into conversation?" Mallory said.

"On the contrary, I picked her up quite deliberately. She was waiting for her boy friend and he was late. I invited her to the party."

"Why did you do that, sir?"

"Because I knew it would be infested by a miserable bunch of stuffed shirts and I thought she might liven things up a bit. She was that sort of girl. Ask Miller, he was paying enough attention to her himself from what I could see. An honest tart. Hair out of a bottle and a skirt that barely covered her backside."

"You were at the party for about twenty minutes before I left," Miller said. "You couldn't have stayed for long."

"About half an hour in all."

"And the girl left with you?"

"You already know that, for Christ's sake." He swung on Mallory. "Are you sure you won't have that drink?"

"No, sir."

"Then I will." He went behind the bar and reached for a bottle. "All of a sudden, things seem to be taking a rather nasty turn."

Mallory ignored the remark. "You say she was here for no more than ten minutes."

"That's right."

"I would have thought she'd have stayed longer."

"If I'd brought her back to sleep with me, the poor little bitch would be alive now, but I didn't."

"Why *did* you bring her back?"

"To pose for me." He swallowed a large whisky and poured himself another. "I offered her five quid to come back and pose for me."

For a brief moment Mallory's composure slipped. He glanced at Miller in bewilderment and Faulkner said, "As it happens I'm a sculptor. That little lot on the dais behind you is a commission I'm working on at the moment for the new Sampson building. The Spirit of Night. This is just a rough draft, so to speak—plaster on wire. I thought a fifth figure might give more balance. I brought Grace back with me to stand up there with the others so I could see."

"And for that you paid her five pounds?"

"Ten, as a matter of fact. I wanted to know and I wanted to know right then. She happened to be available."

"And what did you decide, sir?" Mallory asked.

"I'm still thinking about it. Well, what happens now?"

"Oh, we'll have to make further enquiries, sir," Mallory said. "We'll probably have to see you again, of course, you realise that."

They walked to the door and Faulkner opened it for them. "What about her boy friend, Superintendent? Harold, I think she called him."

"I don't follow you, sir."

Faulkner laughed boyishly. "I suppose I'd better come clean. He arrived just as we were leaving The King's Arms. There was something of a scene. Nothing I couldn't handle, but he was pretty angry—at the girl more than me."

"That's very interesting, sir," Mallory said. "I'll bear it in mind."

He went out. As Miller moved to follow him, Faulkner tapped him on the shoulder. "A private word, Sergeant," he said softly and the smile had left his face. "Stay away from my fiancée in future. One likes to know when a friend is a friend. The trouble with all you bloody coppers is that you're on duty twenty-four hours a day."

There was a sudden viciousness in his voice, but Miller refused to be drawn. "Good night, Mr. Faulkner," he said formally and went out.

Faulkner slammed the door and turned with a frown. For a while he stood there looking thoughtful, then moved back to the drawing board. He removed the clean sheet of cartridge paper, disclosing a sketch of the four statues. After a while he picked up his pencil and started to add an additional figure with bold, sure strokes.

* * *

Outside in the street, it was still raining heavily as Miller and Mallory got into the Chief Superintendent's car where Jack Brady waited with the driver.

"What did you think?" Mallory demanded.

Miller shrugged. "It's hard to say. He's not the sort you meet every day of the week. Did you buy his story about taking the girl back to the studio to pose for him?"

"It's crazy enough to be true, we just can't tell at this stage. He's certainly right about one thing—the girl's boy friend wants checking out." He turned to Brady. "You can handle that one. The fiancé's name is Harold, that's all we know. The girl's father should be able to give you the rest. When you get the address, go straight round and bring him down to Central for questioning."

"What about me, sir?" Miller asked.

"You can go back to that damned party. See Joanna Hartmann and check Faulkner's story. I still don't understand why he left so early. I'll see you at Central as well when you've finished. Get cracking then—I'll drop Brady off."

His car moved away into the rain. Miller watched it go and sighed heavily as he got into the Mini-Cooper. His second visit to Joanna Hartmann's that night was something he didn't fancy one little bit.

8

The party had just about folded and all the guests had departed except for Jack Morgan and Frank Marlowe who sat at the bar with Joanna and her aunt, having a final drink before leaving.

The door bell chimed and Joanna looked up in surprise. "Now, who on earth can that be?"

"Probably Bruno," her aunt remarked acidly. "Returning to tell you that all is forgiven."

"Well, it won't work—not this time." Joanna was annoyed. "He can stew for a while."

There was another ring and Frank Marlowe started to rise. "I'd better go . . ."

"No, I'll handle it. I'll see him myself."

She opened the door, braced for her encounter and found Nick Miller standing there. "Why, Nick," she said in bewilderment.

"Could I come in for a moment?"

"Certainly." She hesitated. "I'm afraid nearly everyone's gone home. We're just having a final drink. Why don't you join us?"

"I'd better not," he said. "To tell you the truth, I'm here on business."

As she closed the door, she stiffened, then turned very slowly. "Bruno? Something has happened to Bruno?"

Miller shook his head quickly. "He's perfectly all right—I've just been speaking to him. There was a girl here earlier—a girl called Grace Packard. He brought her with him, didn't he?"

Jack Morgan got up from his stool and came forward. "That's right, but she left some time ago. Look here, Miller, what is this?"

"As I said, I've already spoken to Faulkner. She went back to his studio with him and left at approximately ten-thirty. She was found by a police officer less than fifteen minutes later in an alley a couple of streets away."

There was a shocked gasp from Mary Beresford and Marlowe said in a whisper, "You mean she's dead?"

"That's right. Murdered. Her neck was broken, probably by a sharp blow from the rear."

"The Rainlover," Mary Beresford said so quietly that it might have been a sigh.

"It could be," Miller said. "On the other hand that kind of killer tends to work to a pattern and it's a little close to his last one." He turned to Morgan. "You've been here all the time?"

"Since I arrived at eighty-thirty or so."

"I can confirm that," Joanna said quickly. "We all can."

"Look here," Marlowe said. "Can we know where we stand? Is this an official call?"

"Just an enquiry." Miller turned to Joanna again. "I understand from your fiancé that he didn't stay very long. Isn't that rather unusual considering that it was your birthday party?"

"Bruno's very much a law unto himself," she said calmly.

Mary Beresford came in under full sail. "Oh, for heaven's sake tell the truth about him for once, Joanna. He didn't stay long because he was asked to leave."

"And why was that?"

"I should have thought it sufficiently obvious. You were here—you saw what happened. He picked that little tart up in a saloon bar and brought her here with the deliberate intention of ruining the party for everyone."

"Aunt Mary—please," Joanna said.

"It's true, isn't it?" The old woman's eyes glittered fiercely. "He arrived dressed like a tramp as usual and with twenty minutes was trying to break the place up."

Miller turned enquiringly. Jack Morgan picked up the two halves of the wooden chopping block that lay on the bar. "Bruno's latest parlour trick."

"Karate?"

"That's right. Imagine what a blow like that would do to somebody's jaw."

A brown belt who was soon to face re-grading to first Dan, Miller could have told him in detail. Instead he looked at Marlowe speculatively. "That bruise on your face—did he do that?"

"Look here," Marlowe said angrily. "I don't know what all this is leading up to, but if you think I'm laying a complaint against him you're mistaken. There was a rather undignified squabble—there usually is when Bruno's around. Nothing more."

"And he left with Grace Packard. You must have found that rather upsetting, Joanna."

"God knows, but she's had enough practice by

now," Mary Beresford said. "You say he took her home with him?"

"That's right, but apparently she only stayed ten minutes or so."

"A likely story."

"Confirmed by the time the body was found. He says that he gave her ten pounds to pose for him. Would you say that was likely?"

Frank Marlowe laughed harshly. "More than that—typical."

Joanna had gone very white, but hung on to her dignity with everything she had left. "As I've already said, he's very much a law unto himself."

"He's been working on a special commission," Jack Morgan said. "One of the most important he's had. It started as a single figure four or five weeks ago and now comprises a group of four. He was discussing with me earlier the question of adding a fifth to give the thing balance."

Miller nodded. "Yes, he did mention that."

"Then why did you have to ask?" Joanna Hartmann said sharply.

Miller frowned. "I'm afraid I don't follow you."

"Are we to take it that my fiancé is under some kind of suspicion in this business?"

"Routine, Joanna, pure routine at the moment. But it has to be done, you must see that surely."

"I don't at all," she said hotly. "What I do see is that you were a guest in my house earlier this evening because I had imagined you a friend."

"Rubbish," Miller said crisply. "You asked me to your party for one reason only. Because my brother is probably the most influential man in Northern Television and you're worried because you've heard there's talk of taking off your series at the end of this season."

"How dare you?" Mary Beresford said. "I'll complain to your superiors."

"You can do what you damned well like," Miller helped himself to a cigarette from a box on the table and smiled calmly. "With my present service and including certain special payments my annual salary at the moment as a Detective Sergeant is one thousand three hundred and eighty-two pounds, Mrs. Beresford. It might interest you to know that every penny of it goes for income tax. Gives me a wonderful feeling of freedom when I'm dealing with people like you."

He turned back to Joanna Hartmann. "Whether you like it or not you've got a few unpleasant facts to face. Number one as far as I'm concerned is that Grace Packard was murdered within an hour of leaving this flat in company with your fiancé, so don't start trying to get on your high horse because we have the impudence to suggest that he might be able to help us with our enquiries."

"I'm Mr. Faulkner's solicitor," Jack Morgan said. "Why wasn't I present when he was questioned?"

"Why not ask him? He was certainly offered the privilege." Miller turned very quickly, moved to the door and opened it. "I'll probably have to see you again, Miss Hartmann," he said formally. "We'd appreciate it if you'd make yourself available during the next couple of days."

"But Miss Hartmann's due in London tomorrow for an important business conference," Frank Marlowe said.

"I can't prevent her going," Miller said, "but it would certainly be a great pity if Faulkner happened to need her and she wasn't here."

He closed the door and chuckled grimly as he went along the corridor to the lift. He'd certainly stirred things up there. It would be more than interesting to see what the outcome, if any, would be.

The heavy silence after Miller had gone out was first broken by Frank Marlowe. "I don't like the smell of this—don't like it at all."

"Neither do I," Jack Morgan said.

Joanna went up the steps to the door, opened a cupboard and took out a sheepskin coat. She pulled it on quickly.

"Did you come in your car, Jack?"

"Yes."

"Good . . . I'd like you to run me round to Bruno's."

Her aunt put a hand on her arm as if she would restrain her. "For goodness' sake, Joanna, don't be a fool. Stay out of this."

Joanna turned on her fiercely. "You don't like him, do you, Aunt Mary. You never did. Because of that you want to believe that he's somehow mixed up in this business. Well, I never will."

The old woman turned away, suddenly looking her age and Frank Marlowe said, "Want me to come?"

Joanna shook her head. "Better not. Would you mind hanging on till we get back?"

"I'll be here."

Jack Morgan opened the door for her and as Joanna turned, her aunt made a final try. "Joanna," she said sharply. "You must listen to me. It's for your own good. Think of your career. You can't afford to get mixed up in the kind of scandal this could cause."

Joanna ignored her completely. "Ready, Jack?" she said and led the way out.

They didn't talk during the drive to Bruno's place, but when Morgan pulled in at the kerb and switched off the engine, she put a hand on his arm.

"You've known Bruno a long time, Jack, longer than any of us. You don't believe he could . . ."

"Not a chance," he told her emphatically. "He's a wild man, I'll give you that, but I couldn't accept the kind of suspicions Nick Miller obviously holds for a moment."

"That's all I wanted to hear." She smiled her relief. "Now let's go up and have a word with him."

But they were wasting their time. There was no reply to their insistent knocking at Bruno's door. After five minutes of fruitless effort, Morgan turned to her and said gently, "Better leave it for now, Joanna. He's probably had enough for one night."

She nodded wearily. "All right, Jack, take me home. We'll try again in the morning. I'll cancel my trip to London."

On the other side of the door, Faulkner listened to the footsteps fade as they descended the stairs. His head was hurting again. My God, but it was hurting. He took a couple of the pills the doctor had given him, poured himself a large whisky and stood at the window and looked out into the night.

Rain spattered against the glass and he rested his aching forehead against it. But it didn't help. Quite suddenly it was as if he was suffocating. Air, that's what he needed—the cold air of night to drive away this terrible pain. He grabbed his trenchcoat and hat and let himself out quickly.

9

"Last time I saw you in the ring was when you fought Terry Jones for the area title," Ma Crowther said. "I thought you had it in your pocket till he gave you that cut over the eye and the ref stopped the fight in the third."

"I always did cut too easily," the Gunner said. "If it hadn't been for that I could have gone right to the top. The Boxing Board took my licence away after the Terry Jones fight on medical advice. Just a vale of tears, isn't it?"

He looked anything but depressed sitting there at the table wearing an old sweater the girl had found him and a pair of boots that had belonged to her father. He had already worked his way through three fried eggs, several rashers of bacon and half a loaf of bread and was now on his third cup of tea.

"You're a funny one and no mistake." Jenny Crowther shook her head. "Doesn't anything ever worry you?"

"Life's too short, darlin'." He helped himself to a cigarette from the old woman's packet. "I shared a cell once with a bloke who was big on this Yoga lark. You've got to learn to relaxez vous. Live for today and use the talents the good Lord's given you."

Jenny laughed helplessly. "I think that's marvellous. Considering the way you make a living."

He wasn't in the least embarrassed. "So I scrounge a few bob where I can. The kind of people I hit can afford it. Insured up to the hilt they are. I don't go around duffing up old women in back street shops."

"The original Robin Hood," she said acidly. "And what happens when someone gets in your way on a job? Do you go quietly or try to smash your way through?"

She piled the dirty dishes on to a tray and went into the kitchen. The Gunner moved across to the fire and sat in the opposite chair to the old woman. "Is she always as sharp as that?"

"She has to be, lad, running an outfit like this."

"You mean she's in charge?"

"Her Dad passed on a couple of months back—cerebral haemorrhage. Jenny was a hairdresser, a good one too, but she dropped that and took over here. Been trying to keep things going ever since."

"Having trouble, then?"

"Only what you'd expect. We've eight drivers and two mechanics and there isn't one who wouldn't take advantage if he could. And then there's the foreman, Joe Ogden. He's the worst of the lot. He's shop steward for the union. Always quoting the book at her, making things as difficult as he can."

"And why would he do that?"

"You've seen her, haven't you?" She poured herself another whisky. "What about you? Where do you go from here?"

He shrugged. "I don't know, Ma. If I can get to the Ring Road I could snatch a lift to any one of a dozen places."

"And then what?" He made no answer and she leaned across and put a hand on his knee. "Don't be a fool, lad. Give yourself up before it's too late."

Which was exactly what the Gunner had been thinking, but he didn't say so. Instead, he got to his feet and grinned. "I'll think about it. In any case there's nothing for you or Jenny to worry about. I'll clear out of here in an hour or so when it's a bit quieter, if that's all right with you."

He went into the kitchen and found the girl at the sink, an apron around her waist, washing the dishes. "Need any help?"

"You can dry if you like."

"Long time since I did this." He picked up a tea towel.

"Even longer before you do it again."

"Heh, what have I done?" he demanded.

"It's just that I can't stand waste," she said. "I mean look at you. Where on earth do you think you're going to go from here? You won't last long out there with every copper for miles around on the watch for you."

"Whose side are you on then?"

"That's another thing. You can't be serious for a moment—not about anything."

She returned to the dishes and the Gunner chuckled. "I'm glad you're angry anyhow."

"What's that supposed to mean?"

"Better than no reaction at all. At least you're interested."

"You'll be lucky. The day I can't do better I'll jump off Queen's Bridge."

But she was smiling and some of the tension had gone out of her when she returned to the washing-up. "I was having an interesting chat with your gran," the Gunner said. "Seems you've got your hands full at the moment."

"Oh, we get by."

"Sounds to me as if you need a good man round the place."

"Why, are you available?"

He grinned. "I wish I was, darlin'."

The judas gate banged outside and steps echoed across the yard. Jenny Crowther frowned. "That's funny, I dropped the latch when I went out earlier."

"Anyone else got a key?"

"Not as far as I know. I'll see who it is. You'd better stay here."

He waited, the kitchen door held open slightly so that he could see what took place. Ma Crowther appeared from the other room and watched as Jenny opened the front door.

The man who pushed his way inside wore a donkey jacket with leather patches on the shoulders and had obviously had a drink. He was hefty enough with arms that were a little too long, but his face was puffed up from too much beer and the weak mouth the biggest giveaway of all.

"And what might you want at this time of night, Joe Ogden?" Ma Crowther demanded.

"Leave this to me, Gran," Jenny said calmly. "Go on now. I'll be in in a minute."

The old woman went back into the sitting-room reluctantly and Jenny closed the door and turned to face Ogden. She held out her hand. "You used a key to open the outside gate. I don't know where you got it from, but I want it."

He smiled slyly. "Nay, lass, I couldn't do that. I like to be able to come and go." He took a step forward and put his hand on the wall so that she was caged in the corner by the sitting-room door. "We could get along just fine, you and me. Why not be sensible? A lass like you's got better things to be doing than trying to run a firm like this. Keeping truckies in their place is man's work."

He tried to kiss her and she twisted her head to one side. "I'm going to give you just five seconds to get out of here. If you don't, I'll send for the police and lay a complaint for assault."

He jumped back as if he had been stung. "You rotten little bitch," he said, his face red and angry. "You won't listen to reason, will you? Well, just remember this—I'm shop steward here. All I have to do is say the word and every man in the place walks out through that gate with me—they'll have no option. I could make things very awkward for you."

She opened the door without a word. He stood there glowering at her, then moved out. "All right, miss," he said viciously. "Don't say I didn't warn you."

She closed the door and turned, shaking with rage. "I'll kill him. I'll kill the bastard," she said and then broke down and sobbed, all the worry and frustration of the weeks since her father's death welling up to the surface.

Strong arms pulled her close and a hand stroked her hair. "Now then, darlin', never say die." She looked up and the Gunner grinned down at her. "Only one way to handle a situation like this. Put the kettle on, there's a good girl. I'll be back in five minutes."

He kissed her full on the mouth and before she could say anything, opened the door and went out into the night.

Joe Ogden paused on the corner, swaying slightly for he was still about three-parts drunk. So she wanted it the hard way did she? Right—then that was the way she could have it. He'd show the bitch—by God he would. By the time he was finished she'd come crawling, begging him to sort things out for her and then he'd call the tune all right.

He crossed the street and turned into a narrow lane, head down against the driving rain, completely absorbed by a series of sexual phantasies in which Jenny Crowther was doing exactly as she was told. The lane was badly lit by a number of old-fashioned gas lamps, long stretches of darkness in between and the pavement was in a bad state of repair, the flags lifting dangerously.

The Gunner descended on him like a thunderbolt in the middle of one of the darker stretches and proceeded to take him apart savagely and brutally in a manner that was as exact as any science.

Ogden cried out in pain as he was propelled into the nearest brick wall with a force that took the breath out of his body. He swung round, aware of the pale blur of a face and swung a fist instinctively, catching the Gunner high on the right cheekbone.

It was the only hit he was to make that night. A boot caught him under the right kneecap, a left and a right screwed into his stomach and a knee lifted into his face as he keeled over, for the Gunner was never one to allow the Queensberry rules to get in his way in this sort of affair.

Ogden rolled over in the rain and the Gunner

kicked him hard about the body half a dozen times, each blow judged to a nicety. Ogden lay there, face against the pavement, more frightened than he had ever been in his life, expecting to meet his end at any moment.

Instead, his assailant squatted beside him in the darkness and said in a strangely gentle voice, "You don't know who I am, but I know you and that's all that matters. Now listen carefully because I'm only going to say this once. You'll get your cards and a week's pay in the post Monday. In the future, you stay away from Crowther's yard. Make any kind of trouble at all, union or otherwise, and I'll get you." He grabbed a handful of Ogden's hair. "Understand?"

"Yes." Ogden could hardly get the word out as fear seized him by the throat.

"See that you do. Now where's the key to the outside gate?"

Ogden fumbled in his left hand pocket, the Gunner took the yale key from him, slammed him back hard against the pavement and walked away.

Ogden got to his knees, dizzy with pain and pulled himself up against the wall. He caught a brief glimpse of the Gunner running through the lighted area under one of the lamps and then he was alone again. Quite suddenly, and for the first time since childhood, he started to cry, dry sobs tearing at his throat as he turned and stumbled away through the darkness.

Crouched by the open doorway in the loft above the old barn in the exact positon the Gunner had occupied earlier, the Rainlover waited patiently, wondering whether the man would return.

The door opened for the second time in ten minutes and the girl appeared, framed against the light, so close that he could see the worry on her face. He started to get up and beyond through the darkness, there was the creaking of the judas gate as it opened. A moment later, the Gunner appeared.

He paused at the bottom of the steps and tossed the key up to Jenny. "This is yours."

She glanced at it briefly. "What happened?"

"Oh, you might say we came to an understanding. He's agreed not to come back. In return he gets his cards and a week's pay, first post Monday morning."

She tilted his head to one side and examined the bruise that was spreading fast under his right eye. "Some understanding. You'd better come in and let me do something about that."

She turned and the Gunner followed her. After he

had closed the door, the yard was dark again, but something moved there in the shadows making no more noise than the whisper of dead leaves brushing across the ground in the autumn. The judas gate creaked slightly and closed with a soft click. In the alley, footfalls faded into the rain.

The Gunner emptied the glass of whisky she had given him with a sigh of satisfaction and turned his head to the light as she gently applied a warm cloth to the bruise under his eye.

"What happened to the old lass, then?"

"I told her to go to bed. It's late."

He glanced at the clock. "You're right. I'll have to be off soon."

"No hurry. You'll stand a better chance later on."

"Maybe you're right."

He was suddenly tired and with the whisky warm in his stomach, contented in a way that he hadn't been for years. It was pleasant there by the cheerful fire with just the one lamp in the corner and the solid, comfortable furniture. She gave him a cigarette and lit a paper spill at the fire for a light.

He took one of the easy chairs and she sat on the rug, her legs tucked underneath her. The Gunner smoked his cigarette slowly from long habit, making it last, and watched her. Strange, but he hadn't felt like this about a woman before. She had everything a man could ever want—a body to thank God for, a pleasant face, strength, character. He pulled himself up short. This was beginning to get out of hand. Trouble was it had been so damned long since he'd been within smelling distance of a bird that probably one of those forty-five-year-old Toms from the back of the market would have looked remarkably like the Queen of the May.

She turned and smiled. "And what's going on inside that ugly skull of yours now?"

"Just thinking how you're about the best-looking lass I've seen in years."

"Not much of a compliment," she scoffed. "Not when you consider where you've been lately."

"Been reading up on me, have you?"

She shrugged. "I caught the final newscast on television. You'd plenty of competition, by the way. There's been a woman murdered earlier tonight on the other side of Jubilee Park."

"Another of these Rainlover things?"

"Who else could it be?" She shivered and added slowly, "When I was alone in the kitchen earlier I got to thinking that maybe that man out there in the yard . . ."

"Was the Rainlover?" The Gunner shook his head emphatically. "Not a chance. The fact that he's seen off this poor bitch earlier is proof enough of that. They always work to a pattern these blokes. Can't help themselves. The chap who jumped you had something a damned sight more old-fashioned on his mind."

She frowned. "I don't know, I was thinking that maybe I should report it to the police."

She hesitated as well she might. Her father had left mother and daughter a business which was worth in cash and property some fifteen thousand pounds yet he had never considered himself as anything other than working class. His daughter was of the same stubborn breed and had been raised to obey the usual working class code which insisted that contact with the police, no matter what the reason, was something to be avoided at all costs.

"And what were you going to tell them?" demanded the Gunner. "That Sean Doyle, with every copper for miles around on his tail, stopped to save you from a fate worse then death, so you fed him and clothed him and sent him on his way rejoicing because you figured you owed him something?" He chuckled harshly. "They'll have you in a cell in Holloway before you know what's hit you."

She sighed. "I suppose you're right."

"Of course I am." With some adroitness he changed the subject. "So I was on the telly, was I?"

"Oh, they did quite a feature on the great Gunner Doyle."

"Free publicity is something I can always use. I hope they mentioned I was the best second-storey man in the North of England."

"Amongst other things, including the fact that you were the most promising middleweight since the war, a contender for the crown until women and booze and fast cars got in the way. They said you were the biggest high-liver the ring had seen since somebody called Jack Johnson."

"Now there's a compliment if you like."

"Depends on your point of view. The commentator said that Johnson had ended up in the gutter without a penny. They seemed to be drawing some kind of comparison."

There was a cutting edge to her voice that needled the Gunner and he said hotly, "Well just for the record, darlin', there's a few things they've missed out like the way I cut so badly that refs used to stop fights I was winning because they'd get worried about the blood pouring all over my face. In that last fight with Terry Jones I got cut so much I was two weeks in hospital. I even needed plastic surgery. They took my licence away so I couldn't box any more. Any idea how I felt?"

"Maybe it was rough, Gunner, life often is, but it didn't give you a licence to steal."

"Nay, lass, I don't need any excuses." He grinned. "I had a few sessions with a psychiatrist at the Scrubs first time I got nicked. He tried to make out that I'd gone bent to get my own back on society."

"What's your version?"

"Chance, darlin', time and chance, that's what happened to me. When the fight game gave me up I'd about two hundred quid in the bank and I was qualified to be just one thing. A bloody labourer. Anything seemed better than that."

"So you decided to try crime?"

"Not really. It just sort of happened. I was staying in the Hallmark Hotel in Manchester, trying to keep up appearances while I tried to con my way into a partnership with a bloke I knew who was running a gambling club. When the deal folded, I was so broke

I couldn't even pay the bill. One night I noticed a bloke in the bar with a wallet full of fivers. Big bookie in from the races."

He stared into the fire, silent for a moment and as he started to speak again, she realised that in some strange way he was re-living that night in every detail.

"He was staying on the same floor as me five rooms along. There was a ledge outside my window, only about a foot wide mind you, but it was enough. I've always had a head for heights ever since I was a kid, always loved climbing. I don't know, maybe if things had been different I might have been a real climber. North face of the Eiger and all that sort of stuff. Those are the blokes with the real guts."

"What happened?" she said.

"I worked my way along the ledge at about two in the morning, got in through his window and lifted the wallet and him snoring the whole time."

"And you got away with it?"

"No trouble at all. Just over six hundred nicker. I ask you, who'd have gone labouring after a touch like that? My fortune was made. As I said, I've always had a head for heights and that kind of thing is a good number. You don't need to work with anyone else which lowers the chance of getting nicked."

"They got you though, didn't they?"

"Twice, that's all, darlin'. Once when I fell forty feet at the back of the Queen's Hotel in Leeds and broke a leg. The second time was when I got nicked at that new hotel in the Vandale Centre. Seems they had one of these electronic eyes switched on. The scuffers were in before I knew what hit me. Oh, I gave them quite a chase over the roofs, but it was all for laughs. I'd been recognised for one thing."

He yawned and shook his head slightly, suddenly very, very tired. "Better get moving I suppose. You don't want me hanging round here in the morning."

The cigarette dropped from his hand to the carpet. She picked it up and tossed it into the fire and the Gunner sighed, leaning back in the comfortable old chair. Very softly Jenny Crowther got up and reached for the rug that was draped over the back of the settee.

As she covered the Gunner, his hand slid across her thigh and he said softly, "Best looking lass I've seen in years."

She didn't move, aware that he was already asleep, but gently disengaged his hand and tucked it under the rug. She stood there for quite a while looking down at that reckless face, almost childlike in repose. In spite of the scar tissue around the eyes and the permanently swollen cheekbones, it was handsome enough, a man's face whatever else he was and her thigh was still warm where he had touched her.

Perhaps it was as well that sleep had overtaken him so suddenly before things had taken their inevitable course—although she would have had no particular objections to that in principle. By no means promiscuous, she was like most young people of her generation, a product of her day and the sexual morality of earlier times meant nothing to her.

But loving, even in that sense, meant some kind of involvement and she couldn't afford that. Better that he should go after an hour or two's sleep. She turned off the light and went and stood at the window, her face against the cold glass, rain hammering hard against it, wondering what would happen to him, wondering where he would run to.

10

Narcia Place lay in an area that provided the local police force with one of its biggest headaches. The streets followed each other upon a pattern that was so exact as to be almost macabre. Sooty plane trees and solid terrace houses, once the homes of the lower middle classes on their way up, but now in multiple occupation due to an influx of immigrants since the war. Most of the whites had left. Those who found it impossible stayed and hated.

It was almost 12:15 when Jack Brady arrived in a Panda car provided by the local station. The whole street was dark and still in the heavy rain and when he rapped the old-fashioned cast-iron knocker on the door of number ten there was no immediate response. The driver of the Panda car vanished into the entry that led to the back yard without a word and Brady tried again.

It was at least five minutes before a window was pushed up above his head and a voice called, "What the hell you think you're playing at this time in the morning?"

"Police," Brady replied. "Open up and be sharp about it. I haven't got all night."

The window went down and the driver of the Panda car emerged from the entry. "Any joy?"

"Just stuck his head out of the window," Brady said. "Get round to the back yard, just in case he tries to scarper."

But there was no need for at that moment, the bolt was drawn and the front door opened. Brady pushed it back quickly and went in. "Harold Phillips?"

"That's me—what is this?"

His feet were bare and he wore an old raincoat. Brady looked him over in silence and Harold swallowed, his black eyes flickering restlessly. He looked hunted and was very obviously scared.

Brady smiled in an avuncular manner and put a hand on his shoulder. "I'm afraid I've got some bad news for you, son. I understand you're engaged to be married to a Miss Grace Packard?"

"That's right." Harold went very still. "What's happened? She been in an accident or something?"

"Worse than that, son. She was found dead earlier tonight in an alley called Dob Court on the other side of Jubilee Park."

Harold stared at him for a long moment, then started to puke. He got a hand to his mouth, turned and fled into the kitchen. Brady found him leaning over the sink, a hand on the cold water tap.

After a while Harold turned, wiping his mouth with the back of one hand. "How did it happen?"

"We're not certain. At the moment it looks as if her neck was broken."

"The Rainlover?" The words were almost a whisper.

"Could be."

"Oh, my God." Harold clenched a fist convulsively. "I had a date with her tonight. We were supposed to be going dancing."

"What went wrong?"

"I was late. When I turned up she'd got involved with another bloke."

"And she went off with him." Harold nodded. "Do you know who he was?"

Harold shook his head. "Never seen him before,

but the landlord seemed to know him. That's the landlord of The King's Arms near Regent Square."

"What time was this?"

"About half-eight."

"Did you come straight home afterwards?"

"I was too upset so I walked around in the rain for a while. Then I had a coffee in the buffet at the railway station. Got home about half-nine. Me mum was in bed so I took her a cup of tea and went myself."

"Just you and your mother live here?"

"That's right."

"She goes to bed early then?"

"Spends most of her time there these days. She isn't too well."

Brady nodded sympathetically. "I hope we haven't disturbed her."

Harold shook his head. "She's sleeping like a baby. I looked in on my way down." He seemed much more sure of himself now and a strange half-smile played around his mouth like a nervous tic that couldn't be controlled. "What happens now?"

"I'd like you to come down to Central if you wouldn't mind, just to have a few words with Chief Superintendent Mallory—he's in charge of the case. The girl's father is already there, but we need all the assistance we can get. You could help a lot. Give us details of her friends and interests, places she would be likely to visit."

"Glad to," Harold said. "I'll go and get dressed. Only be five minutes."

He went out and the Panda driver offered Brady a cigarette. "Quite a technique you have. The silly bastard thinks he's got you eating out of his hand."

"Glad you noticed," Brady said, accepting the cigarette and a light. "We'll make a copper out of you yet."

There was a white pill box on the mantelpiece and he picked it up and examined the label. It carried the name of a chemist whose shop was no more than a couple of streets away. *The Capsules—one or two according to instructions—it is dangerous to exceed the stated dose.*

Brady opened the box and spilled some of the white and green capsules into his palm. "What you got there?" the Panda man demanded.

"From the look of them I'd say it's what the doctor gave my wife last year when she burnt her hand and couldn't sleep for the pain. Canbutal. Half a dozen of these and you'd be facing your Maker."

He replaced the box on the mantelpiece, a slight frown on his face. "Tell you what," he said to the Panda driver. "You go and wait for us in the car and bang the door as hard as you like on the way out."

The young constable, old before his years and hardened to the vagaries of C.I.D. men, left without a word, slamming the door so hard that the house shook. Brady went and stood at the bottom of the stairs, but heard no sound until a door opened and Harold appeared buttoning his jacket on the way down.

"What was all that then?" he demanded. "Thought the house was falling down."

"Just my driver on his way out to the car. I think the wind caught the door. Ready to go?"

"Whenever you are." Harold took down his raincoat and struggled into it as he made for the door. "Fame and fortune here I come. Who knows, I might be selling my story to the *Sunday News* before I'm finished."

With an effort of will, Brady managed to stop himself from assisting him down the steps with a boot in the backside. Instead he took a deep breath and closed the door behind him with infinite gentleness. He was beginning to feel sorry for Harold's mother.

It was chance more than anything else that led Miller to The King's Arms after leaving Joanna Hartmann's flat. His quickest route back to Central C.I.D. took him along Lazer Street and the pub stood on the corner. It was the light in the rear window which caused him to brake suddenly. The landlord would have to be interviewed sooner or later to confirm the circumstances of Grace Packard's meeting with Faulkner and Morgan, but there was no reason why that couldn't wait till morning.

The real truth was that Miller was more interested in the disturbance that had taken place, the trouble with the girl's boy friend which Faulkner had hinted at. "Nothing I couldn't handle," he had said. The sort of phrase Miller would have expected from some back street tearaway, indicating a pattern of violence unusual and disturbing in a man of Faulkner's education and background.

He knocked on the back door and after a while it was opened on a chain and Harry Meadows peered out. He grinned his recognition for they were old friends.

"What's this then, a raid?"

Miller went in as Meadows unchained the door. "A few words of wisdom, Harry, that's all."

"Nothing stronger?"

"Only if you've got a cup of tea to put it in."

"Coming up."

Miller unbuttoned his coat and went across to the fire. The kitchen was large, but cluttered with crates of bottled beer and cases of whisky. It was warm and homely with the remains of the supper still on the table and the old sofa on the other side of the fireplace looked very inviting.

"See you've got another killing on your hands," Meadows said as he came back into the room with a mug of tea.

"Where did you hear that?"

"Late night news on the radio. Not that they were giving much away. Just said the body of a woman had been found near Jubilee Park."

"Dob Court to be precise." Miller swallowed some of his tea, coughing as the whisky in it caught at the back of his throat.

"Dob Court? That's just round the corner from here." Meadows looked grim. "Was it anyone I knew?"

"A girl called Grace Packard."

Meadows stared at him, the skin tightening visibly across his face. Quite suddenly he went to the sideboard, opened a bottle of brandy and poured a large dose into the nearest glass. He swallowed it down and turned, shuddering.

"She was in here earlier tonight."

"I know, Harry, that's why I'm here. I understand there was some trouble."

Meadows helped himself to another brandy. "This is official then?"

"Every word counts so take your time."

Meadows was looking a lot better as the brandy took effect. He sat down at the table. "There's a bloke called Faulkner comes in here a lot. Only lives a couple of streets away. He was in here earlier tonight with a friend of his, a solicitor called Morgan. Nice bloke. He handled the lease of this place for me when I decided to buy last year."

"What time did they come in?"

"Somewhere around half-eight."

"Who else was here?"

"Nobody. Trade's been so bad in the evenings since this Rainlover business started that I've had to lay off the bar staff."

"I see. When did the girl arrive?"

"About five minutes after the other two."

"You knew her name, so presumably she'd been in before?"

"Two or three times a week, usually with a different bloke and she wasn't too particular about their ages either."

"Was she a Tom?"

"That's the way it looked to me."

"And what about this boy friend of hers?"

"You mean Harold?" Meadows shrugged. "He's met her in here maybe half a dozen times. I don't even know his second name."

"Was he picking up her earnings?"

"Could be, I suppose. He didn't look so tough to me, but you can never tell these days."

Miller nodded. "All right, what happened between Faulkner and the girl?"

"She sat on a stool at one end of the bar and he told me to give her a drink. It seems he and Morgan were going on to some posh do and Faulkner got the idea it might be fun to take the girl. She must have liked the idea because they all left together."

"And then Harold arrived."

"That's right and he didn't like what he found. Ended up taking a punch at Faulkner who got very nasty with him. I had to intervene. In fact I told Morgan to tell him he needn't come back. I've had about as much as I can take."

"He's been mixed up in this sort of trouble before then?"

"Too damned much for my liking. When he loses his temper he's a raving madman, that one. Doesn't know what he's doing. He was in here one Saturday night a couple of months back and a couple of market porters came in. You know what they're like—rough lads—they started taking the mickey out of his posh voice and so on. He took them both out in the alley, gave them a hell of a beating."

"Did you report it?"

"Come off it, Mr. Miller. I've got the reputation of the house to think of. I only put up with him because most of the time he's a real gent and why should I cry over a couple of tearaways like that? They asked for it, they got it."

"A point of view." Miller started to button his coat. "Strange in a man of his background, all this violence."

Meadows hesitated perceptibly. "Look, I don't know if this is any use to you, but he was in here on his own one night, not exactly drunk, but well on the way. We were talking about some court case in the evening paper. Three blokes who'd smashed up an old-age pensioner for the three or four quid that was in her purse. I said blokes like that were the lowest form of animal life. He leaned across the bar and took me by the tie. 'No, they're not, Harry,' he said. 'The lowest form of animal life is a screw.' "

In other days the man who turned the key in the lock had been called a warder. In more enlightened times he was known as a prison officer, but to anyone who had ever served time he was a screw, hated and despised.

"You think he's been inside?" Miller said.

Meadows shrugged. "Sounds crazy, I know, but I've reached the stage where I could believe anything about that one." He opened the door. "You don't think he killed Grace Packard, do you?"

"I haven't the slightest idea. What happened to Harold after the others left, by the way? You didn't tell me that."

"I offered him a drink and he told me where to go and went out after them. Funny thing was he turned up again about five minutes afterwards full of apologies. Said he was sorry he'd lost his temper and so on. Then he tried to get Faulkner's address out of me."

"He knew his name then?"

"Apparently he'd heard me use it during the fuss when I called out to Faulkner to lay off."

"Did you give him the address?"

"Do I look as if I came over on a banana boat?" Meadows shrugged. "Mind you, there's always the telephone book."

"As you say." Miller punched him lightly in the shoulder. "See you soon, Harry."

He went. Crossed the yard through the heavy rain.

Meadows watched him climb into the Cooper, then closed the door.

Miller went up the steps of the Central Railway Station and paused to light a cigarette in the porch. The match flared in his cupped hands briefly illuminating the white face and dark eyes. Here and there in the vast concourse a lounger stiffened, turned and faded briskly into the night which was no more than Miller had intended for the railway station of any great city is the same the world over, a happy hunting ground for wrongdoers of every description.

He moved across to the buffet by the ticket barrier and looked in through the window. The young woman he was searching for was sitting on a stool at one end of the tea bar. She saw him at once, for there were few things in life that she missed, and came out.

She was about twenty-five years of age with a pleasant, open face and her neat tweed suit was in excellent taste. She might have been a schoolteacher or someone's private secretary. In fact she had appeared before the local bench on no fewer than five occasions for offences involving prostitution and had recently served three months in a detention centre.

She nodded familiarly. "'Evening, Mr. Miller, or should I say good morning?"

"Hello, Gilda. You must be hard up to turn out on a night like this with a bloody maniac hanging around out there in the rain."

"I can look after myself." When she lifted her umbrella he saw that the ferrule had been sharpened into a wicked-looking steel point. "Anyone makes a grab at me gets this through the eyes."

Miller shook his head. "You think you can take on the whole world, don't you? I wonder what you'll look like ten years from now."

"Just older," she said brightly.

"If you're lucky, only by then you'll be down to a different class of customer. Saturday night drunks at a quid a time for a quickie round the back of the station."

She wasn't in the least offended. "We'll see. What was it you wanted?"

"I suppose you heard there was a girl killed earlier tonight?"

"That's right. Other side of the park, wasn't it?"

"Her name was Grace Packard. I've been told she was on the game. Is that true?"

Gilda showed no particular surprise. "Kinky looking little tart, all plastic mac and knee boots."

"That's it."

"She tried working the station about six months ago. Got herself into a lot of trouble."

"What kind?"

"Pinching other people's regulars, that sort of thing. We moved her on in the end."

"And how did you manage that?" She hesitated and he said harshly, "Come on, Gilda, this is murder."

"All right," she said reluctantly. "I asked Lonny Brogan to have a word with her. She took the point."

"I can imagine she would after hearing what that big ape had to say," Miller said. "One other thing, did anyone pimp for her?"

Gilda chuckled contemptuously. "Little half-baked kid with a face like the underbelly of a fish and black sideboards. Harold something or other. Christ knows what she saw in him."

"You saw her give him money?"

"Plenty of times—mostly to get rid of him from what I could see."

He nodded. "All right, Gilda, I'll be seeing you."

"Oh, Mr. Miller," she said reprovingly. "I hope you don't mean that the way it sounds."

Her laughter echoed mockingly from the vaulted ceiling as he turned and walked away.

11

When Brady and Harold entered the general office at Central C.I.D. it was bustling with activity for no man might reasonably expect to see his bed on a night like this. Brady left Harold on an uncomfortable wooden bench with the Saturday sport's paper and went in to Chief Superintendent Mallory who was using Grant's office.

Mallory was shaving with a battery-operated electric razor and reading a report at the same time. His white shirt was obviously fresh on and he looked crisp and alert in spite of the hour.

"I've got the girl's boy friend outside," Brady said. "Phillips his name is—Harold Phillips."

"What's your first impression?"

"Oh, there's something there all right. For a start, he's an unpleasant little bastard."

"You can't hang a man for that."

"There's a lot more to it than that."

Brady gave him the gist of his conversation with Harold and when he was finished, Mallory nodded. "All right, let's have him in."

When Brady called him, Harold entered with a certain bravado and yet his nervousness was betrayed in the muscle that twitched in his right cheek.

Mallory greeted him with extreme politeness. "Good of you to come at this hour, Mr. Phillips. We appreciate it."

Harold's confidence received a king-size boost and he sat down in the chair Brady brought forward and gave Mallory a big man-of-the-world smile. "Anything I can do, Superintendent. You've only got to say."

Brady offered him a cigarette. As he was lighting it, there was a knock on the door and Miller glanced in. He was about to withdraw, but Mallory shook his head and beckoned him inside. Miller closed the door behind him and took up a position by the window without a word.

"Now then, sir, just to get the record straight, you are Mr. Harold Phillips of 10, Narcia Place?" Mallory began.

"That's me."

"I'm given to understand that you and Miss Grace Packard were engaged to be married. Is that correct?"

"I suppose you could say that in a way." Harold shrugged. "I bought her a ring a couple of months back, but nothing was really official. I mean we hadn't set a date or anything."

"I understand, sir. Now I wonder if you'd mind going over the events of last night again. I know you've already discussed this with Constable Brady, but it would help me to hear for myself."

"Well, as I told Mr. Brady, I had a date with Grace at half-eight."

"Just one moment, sir. What happened before that? What time did you get home from work?"

Harold smiled bravely. "To tell you the truth I'm not actually working at the moment, Superintendent. It's my back you see. I had this accident about a year ago so I have to be very careful."

Mallory looked sympathetic. "That must be difficult for you. You were saying that you had an appointment with Miss Packard at eight-thirty?"

"That's right. In The King's Arms, the one near Regent Square on the corner of Lazer Street."

"And you kept that appointment?"

"I was a couple of minutes late. When I got there she was leaving with two blokes."

"Who were they?"

"I don't know—never seen 'em before."

"Did she often do this sort of thing?"

Harold sighed heavily. "I'm afraid she did. She was sort of restless, if you know what I mean. Always looking for something new."

It sounded like a line from a bad television play, but Mallory simply nodded and went on, "What happened when you arrived and found her leaving with these two men?"

"I tried to stop her, tried to reason with her, but she wouldn't listen." Harold flushed. "Then one of them got hold of me—great big bloke he was. He twisted my hand in one of these judo locks or something. Put me down on my face. That's when the landlord moved in and told 'em to clear off."

"And what did you do then, sir?"

Harold frowned as if trying to remember. "Oh, had a drink with the landlord—on the house."

"Did you go straight home afterwards?"

"No, like I told Mr. Brady, I was too upset. I walked around in the rain for a while, then I had a coffee in the station buffet. Got home about half-nine. Me mum was in bed so I took her a cup of tea and went myself."

Mallory had been making notes. He added a sentence and as he glanced up, Miller said, "Excuse me, sir, I've been expecting a message."

He went out into the main office, picked up the telephone on his desk and rang through to Mallory. "Miller here, sir. He's lying."

"That's certainly nice to know," Mallory said calmly. "I'll be straight out."

He put down his phone and smiled brightly at Harold. "I'll only be a moment." He got to his feet and said to Brady, "See that Mr. Phillips gets a cup of tea, will you, Constable? There should be some left in the pot."

He found Miller sitting on the edge of his desk drinking someone else's coffee. Mallory sat down in the chair and started to fill his pipe. "Nasty little bastard, isn't he?"

"He may have his moments, but they must be few and far between," Miller said. "To start with I've seen Harry Meadows, the landlord of The King's Arms. After the fuss, he offered Harold a drink on the house. Harold told him to get stuffed and went off after the others. Five minutes later he returned full of apologies to claim his free glass."

"Now why would he do that?" Mallory said thoughtfully.

"Apparently he spent the time trying to pump Meadows. Wanted to know where Faulkner lived."

"You mean he actually knew Faulkner by name?"

"Oh, yes, he made that clear enough. He'd heard Meadows use it during the argument."

Mallory grinned like the Cheshire cat, the first time Miller had ever seen him smile. "Well that's a nice fat juicy lie he's told us for a start."

"There's more," Miller said. "Grace Packard was on the game. Worked the station until the rest of the girls moved her on a month or two back. According to my informant she had a boy friend who picked up her earnings pretty regularly. The description fits our Harold exactly."

Mallory got to his feet. "Let's go back in."

Harold was half-way through his third cigarette and glanced round nervously when the door opened. "Sorry about that, Mr. Phillips," Mallory said. He smiled heartily and held out his hand. "Well, I don't think we need to detain you any longer. You can go back to bed now."

Harold's mouth gaped. "You mean you don't need me any more?"

"That's right. The information you've given us will be most helpful. I can't thank you enough for turning out at this hour in the morning. It's that kind of co-operation that helps us beat these things you know." He turned to Brady who came to attention briskly. "See that Mr. Phillips gets home will you, Constable?"

"See to it myself, sir." Brady put a hand under Harold's elbow, looking more avuncular than ever. "Have you home in fifteen minutes, sir."

Harold grinned. "Be seeing you, Superintendent," he said and went out of the room like a turkey-cock.

Mallory sat down and put a match to his pipe. "No harm in letting him think he's out of the wood for a few hours. When we pull him in again in the morning the shock will just about cripple him."

"You really think he's got something to hide, sir?" Miller demanded.

"He's lying when he says he doesn't know Faulkner by name—that's for a start. Then there's this business about the girl—the fact that he was pimping for her."

"It still doesn't add up to murder."

"It never does to start with, Sergeant. Suppositions, inaccuracies, statements that don't really hold water—that's all we ever have to work with in most cases. For example, Phillips says that he walked the streets for a while after leaving the pub, then had a coffee at the station buffet. How many people would you say use that buffet on a Saturday night?"

"Thousands, sir."

"Exactly. In other words it would be unreasonable to expect some sort of personal identification by any of the buffet staff. Another thing—as far as we can judge at the moment, the girl was killed at around half-ten."

"And Phillips was home at nine-thirty and in bed ten minutes or so later. What was it he said? That he took his mother a cup of tea?"

"Interesting thing about Mrs. Phillips," Mallory said. "Brady had to kick on the door for a good five minutes before he could rouse Phillips. There wasn't a bleat from the old girl. In fact Phillips told him she was sleeping like a baby."

Miller frowned. "That doesn't make very good sense."

"Even more interesting was the bottle of Canbutal capsules Brady found on the mantelpiece. A couple of those things and you wouldn't hear a bomb go off in the next street."

"Might be an idea to check with her doctor in the morning, just to get a complete picture."

Mallory nodded. "Brady can handle that." He got to his feet. "I'm going over to the Medical School now. We've hauled Professor Murray out of bed. He's going to get cracking on the post-mortem just as soon as the Forensic boys have finished with her. You'd better get a couple of hours' sleep in the rest room. If I want you, I'll phone."

Miller helped him on with his coat. "What about Faulkner?"

Mallory shook his head. "I never had much of a hunch about him, not in the way I do about Phillips."

"I'm afraid I can't agree with you there, sir."

For a moment, Mallory poised on the brink of one of those sudden and terrible wraths for which he was famous. With a great effort he managed to control himself and said acidly, "Don't tell me you're going to solve this thing in a burst of intuitive genius, Miller?"

"Meadows had some very interesting things to say about him, sir," Miller said patiently. "There's a pattern of violence there that just doesn't fit in a man of his background. He uses force too easily, if you follow me."

"So do I when the occasion calls for it," Mallory said. "Is that all you have to go on?"

"Not exactly, sir. He had a pretty strange conversation with Meadows one night when he was drunk. Meadows got the impression that he'd been inside."

Mallory frowned. "Did he indeed? Right, get on to C.R.O. in London. Tell them it's for me. Say I want everything they have on Faulkner by breakfast. I'll discuss it with you then."

The door banged behind him and Miller grinned softly. For a moment there, just for a moment, it had looked as if they were going to clash. That moment would come again because George Mallory was a stubborn man and Nick Miller was a sleeping partner in a business so large that he didn't need to put himself out to anyone for the sake of keeping his job. Not God or even Chief Superintendents from New Scotland Yard. An interesting situation. He lit a cigarette, picked up Mallory's telephone and asked for Information Room.

12

The small rest room was badly overcrowded and there was hardly room to move between the camp beds which had been specially imported. Miller slept badly which was hardly surprising. There was an almost constant disturbance at what seemed like five minute intervals throughout the night as colleagues were sent for and the rain continued to hammer relentlessly against the window pane above his head.

At about seven a.m. he gave up the struggle, got a towel and went along the corridor to the washroom. He stood under a hot shower for a quarter of an hour, soaking the tiredness away and then sampled the other end of the scale, an ice-cold needle spray for precisely thirty seconds just to give himself an appetite.

He was half-way through a plate of bacon and eggs and on his third cup of tea in the canteen when Brady found him. The big Irishman eased himself into the opposite chair and pushed a flimsy across the table.

"Hanley in Information asked me to give you that. Just come in from C.R.O. in London."

Miller read it quickly and took a deep breath. "Quite a lad when he gets going, our Bruno. Where's Mallory?"

"Still at the post-mortem."

Miller pushed back his chair. "I'd better get over to the Medical School then. You coming?"

Brady shook his head. "I still haven't contacted Mrs. Phillips' doctor. Mallory told me to wait till after breakfast. Said there was no rush. I'll be across as soon as I've had a word with him."

"I'll see you then," Miller said and left quickly.

The mortuary was at the back of the Medical School, a large, ugly building in Victorian Gothic with stained glass windows and the vaguely religious air common to the architecture of the period.

Jack Palmer, the Senior Technician, was sitting in his small glass office at the end of the main corridor and he came to the door as Miller approached.

"Try and arrange your murders at a more convenient hour next time will you," he said plaintively. "My first Saturday night out in two months ruined. My wife was hopping mad, I can tell you."

"My heart bleeds for you, Jack," Miller said amiably. "Where's the top brass?"

"Having tea inside. I shouldn't think you rate a cup."

Miller opened the door on the other side of the office and went into the white-tiled hall outside the theatre. Mallory was there, seated at a small wooden table talking to Henry Wade, the Head of Forensic, and Professor Stephen Murray, the University Professor of Pathology, a tall, spare Scot.

Murray knew Miller socially through his brother and greeted him with the familiarity of an old friend. "You still look as if you've stepped straight out of a whisky advert, Nick, even at eight-fifteen in the morning. How are you?"

"Fine—nothing that a couple of weeks' leave wouldn't cure." Miller turned to Mallory. "I've just been handed the report on Faulkner from C.R.O."

"Anything interesting?"

"I think you could say that, sir. Harry Meadows wasn't wrong—he does have a record. Fined twice for assault and then about two years ago he ran amok at some arty Chelsea party."

"Anybody hurt?"

"His agent. Three broken ribs and a fractured jaw. Faulkner's a karate expert so when he loses his temper it can have rather nasty results."

"Did they send him down?"

"Six months and he did the lot. Clocked one of the screws and lost all his remission."

"Anything known against him since?"

"Not a thing. Apparently some sort of psychiatric investigation was carried out when he was inside so there's quite an interesting medical report. Should be along soon."

Mallory seemed curiously impatient. "All right, all right, we'll talk about it later." He turned to Professor Murray. "What do you think then, is this another Rainlover thing or isn't it?"

"That's for you to decide," Murray said. "I'm the last man to make that kind of prediction—I've been at this game too long. If you mean are there any obvious differences between this murder and the others, all I can say is yes and leave you to form your own conclusions."

"All right, Professor, fire away."

Murray lit a cigarette and paced up and down restlessly. "To start with the features which are similar. As in all the other cases, the neck was broken cleanly with a single powerful blow, probably a blunt instrument with a narrow edge."

"Or the edge of the hand used by an expert," Miller suggested.

"You're thinking of karate, I suppose," Murray smiled faintly. "Always possible, but beware of trying to make the facts fit your own suppositions, Nick. A great mistake in this game, or so I've found."

"What other similarities were present, Professor?" Mallory asked, obviously annoyed at Miller's interruption.

"No physical ones. Time, place, weather—that's what I was meaning. Darkness and rain—the lonely street."

"And the features in this one that don't fit?" Henry Wade said. "What about those?"

"Recent bruising on the throat, another bruise on the right cheek as if someone had first grabbed her angrily around the neck and then struck her a violent blow, probably with his fist. The death blow came afterwards. Now this is a very real departure. In the other cases, there was no sign of violence except in the death blow itself. Quick, sharp, clean, obviously totally unexpected."

"And in this case the girl obviously knew what was coming," Mallory said.

Henry Wade shook his head. "No, I'm afraid that won't work, sir. If she was attacked by an unknown assailant, she'd have put up some sort of a struggle, even if it was only to get her nails to his face. We didn't find any signs that would indicate that such a struggle took place."

"Which means that she stood there and let someone knock her about," Mallory said. "Someone she knew."

"I don't see how we can be certain of that, sir." Miller couldn't help pointing out what seemed an obvious flaw. "She was on the game after all. Why couldn't she have been up that alley with a potential customer?"

Again the irritation was noticeable in Mallory's voice. "Would she have stood still while he grabbed her throat, fisted her in the face? Use your intelligence, Sergeant. It's quite obvious that she took a beating from someone she was perfectly familiar with and she took it because she was used to it."

"I think the Superintendent's got a point, Nick," Henry Wade said. "We're all familiar with the sort of relationship a prostitute has with her minder. Beatings are the order of the day, especially when the pimp thinks his girl isn't coughing up all her earnings and the women take their hidings quietly, too. God knows why. I suppose a psychiatrist would have an answer."

"True enough," Miller admitted.

"And there's one important point you're forgetting," Wade added. "In every Rainlover case yet he's always taken some memento. Either an article of clothing or a personal belonging. That doesn't seem to have happened here."

"Anything else, Miller?" Mallory enquired.

"Was there any cash in her handbag, sir?"

"Two or three pounds in notes and silver."

"Faulkner said he gave her a ten-pound note."

"Exactly, Sergeant." Mallory gave him a slight, ironic smile. "Any suggestions as to what happened to it?"

"No, sir." Miller sighed. "So we're back to Harold Phillips?"

"That's right and I want him pulled in now. You can take Brady with you."

"And Faulkner, sir?"

"Oh, for God's sake, Sergeant, don't you ever take no for an answer?"

There was an electric moment and then Murray

cut in smoothly. "All very interesting, gentlemen, but you didn't allow me to finish my story. If it's of any use to you, the girl had intercourse just before her death."

Mallory frowned. "No suggestion of rape, is there?"

"None whatsoever. In view of the conditions I would say the act took place against the wall and definitely with her consent. Of course one can't judge whether under threat or not."

Mallory got to his feet. "Only another nail in his coffin." He turned to Miller. "Go and get Phillips now and bring the clothes he was wearing last night. I'll expect you back within half an hour."

There was a time to argue and a time to go quietly. Miller went without a word.

Miller met Brady coming down the steps of the main entrance of the Town Hall. "You look as if you've lost a quid and found a tanner," he told Miller. "What's up?"

"We've got to pull Harold Phillips in right away. Mallory thinks he's the mark."

"Harold—the Rainlover?" Brady said incredulously.

Miller shook his head. "Could be this wasn't a

Rainlover killing, Jack. There were differences—I'll explain on the way."

"Did you and Mallory have a row or something?" Brady asked as they went down the steps to the Mini-Cooper.

"Not quite. He's got the bit between his teeth about Harold and I just don't see it, that's all."

"And what about Faulkner?"

"The other side of the coin. Mallory thinks exactly as I do about Harold."

"He could change his mind," Brady said as they got in the car. "I've just seen a report from Dwyer, the beat man who found the body and got slugged."

"How is he?" Miller said as he switched on the ignition and drove away.

"A bit of concussion, that's all. They're holding him in the infirmary for observation. There's an interesting titbit for you in his report though. Says that about ten minutes before finding the body, he bumped into a bloke leaving the coffee stall in Regent Square."

"Did he recognise him?"

"Knows him well—local resident. A Mr. Bruno Faulkner."

The Mini-Cooper swerved slightly as Miller glanced at him involuntarily. "Now that is interesting."

He slowed suddenly, turning the car into the next street and Brady said, "Now where are we going? This isn't the way to Narcia Street."

"I know that coffee stall," Miller said. "Run by an old Rugby pro called Sam Harkness. He usually closes about nine on a Sunday morning after catching the breakfast trade."

Brady shook his head sadly. "Mallory is just going to love you for this. Ah well, a short life and a merry one." He eased back in the seat and started to fill his pipe.

Rain drifted across Regent Square in a grey curtain and when Miller braked to a halt, there were only two customers at the coffee stall, all-night taxi drivers eating fried egg sandwiches in the shelter of the canopy. Miller and Brady ran through the rain and Harkness turned from the stove, a frying pan in his hand.

"Oh, it's you, Mr. Miller. Looking for breakfast?"

"Not this time, Sam," Miller said. "Just a little information. You know about last night's murder in Dob Court?"

"Don't I just? Cars around here most of the night. Did all right out of it in tea and wads, I can tell you."

"I've just been looking at Constable Dwyer's report on what happened. He says he called here about ten past ten."

"That's right."

"I understand you had a customer who was just leaving—a Mr. Bruno Faulkner according to Dwyer."

Harkness nodded and poured out a couple of teas. "Artist. Lives round the corner from here. Regular customer of mine. Turns out at any old time in the a.m. when he's run out of fags. You know what they're like, these blokes."

"And it was cigarettes he wanted last night was it?" Brady asked.

"He bought twenty Crown King-size. As a matter of fact I'm waiting for him to look in again. He left a pair of gloves—lady's gloves."

He searched under the counter and produced them. They were in imitation black leather, heavily decorated with pieces of white plastic and diamanté, cheap and ostentatious—the sort of thing that was to be found in any one of a dozen boutiques which had sprung up in the town of late to cater for the needs of young people.

"Rather funny really," Harkness said. "He pulled them out of his pocket when he was looking for change. I said they were hardly his style. He seemed a bit put out to me. Tried to make out they were his fiancée's, but that was just a load of cobblers if you ask me. She's been here with him—his fiancée I mean—Joanna Hartmann. You see her on the telly all the time. Woman like that wouldn't wear this sort of rubbish."

Amazing how much people told you without being asked. Miller picked up the gloves. "I'll be seeing Mr. Faulkner later this morning, Sam. I'll drop these in at the same time."

"Probably still in bed with the bird they belong to," Harkness called. "Bloody artists. I should be so lucky."

"So Faulkner had Grace Packard's gloves in his pocket," Brady said when they got back to the Mini-Cooper. "So what? He didn't deny having her at his flat. He'll simply say she left the gloves by mistake or something."

Miller handed him the gloves, took out his wallet and produced a pound note. "This is on me, Jack. Take a taxi to the Packard house. I don't suppose the mother's in too good a state, but see if the father can give you a positive identification on those gloves. Come straight on to Narcia Street from there. I'll be waiting for you."

"Mallory isn't going to like this."

"That's just too bloody bad. How far did you get with Mrs. Phillips' doctor?"

"He wouldn't discuss it on the phone. It's that Indian bloke—Lal Das. You know what these wogs are like. Give 'em an inch and they'll take a mile every time."

"All right, Jack, all right, I'll see him myself," Miller said, an edge to his voice for the kind of racial prejudice that seemed to be part of the make-up of so many otherwise decent men like Brady was guaranteed to bring out the worst in him.

"Half an hour then," Brady said, checking his watch. "That's all it should take."

"I'll wait for you outside." Miller watched him run across to one of the taxis, got into the Mini-Cooper and drove away quickly.

13

Lal Das, to whom Brady had referred so contemptuously, was a tall, cadaverous Indian. A Doctor of Medicine and a Fellow of the Royal College of Physicians, he could have secured a senior post in a major hospital any time he wanted and yet he preferred to run a large general practice in one of the less salubrious parts of the city. He had a national reputation in the field of drug addiction and, in this connection, Miller had frequently sought his advice.

The Indian had just finished breakfast and was working his way through the Sunday supplements when Miller was shown in. Das smiled and waved him to a seat. "Just in time for coffee."

"Thanks very much."

"Business or did you just happen to be in the neighbourhood?"

Miller took the cup of coffee the Indian handed to him and shook his head. "You had a call earlier—a query concerning a Mrs. Phillips of 10, Narcia Street."

The Indian nodded. "That's right. The officer who spoke to me wasn't terribly co-operative. Wouldn't tell me what the whole thing was about, so I simply refused to give him the information he required until I knew more about it. A doctor/patient relationship can only function satisfactorily when there is an atmosphere of complete trust. I would only be prepared to discuss a patient's case history and private affairs in exceptional circumstances."

"Would murder be extreme enough?" Miller asked.

Lal Das sighed and put down his cup carefully. "I think you'd better tell me about it. I'll judge for myself."

"Fair enough. The man at the centre of things is the woman's son—Harold Phillips. Presumably he's a patient of yours also?"

An expression of real distaste crossed the Indian's face. "For my sins. A particularly repellant specimen of present-day youth."

"He had a girl friend called Grace Packard. Ever meet her?"

Das shook his head. "I notice you use the past tense."

"She was murdered last night. Naturally Harold was called upon to explain his movements, especially as he'd had some sort of row with her earlier in the evening. His story is that he was home by nine-thirty. He says that his mother was in bed and that he took her a cup of tea and went himself.

"So his mother is his alibi?"

"That's about the size of it. The murder was committed around ten-fifteen you see."

Das nodded. "But what is it you want from me? Surely it's straightforward enough."

"It might have been if something rather strange hadn't occurred. Two police officers went to Narcia Street just after midnight to bring Harold in for questioning. They had to kick on the door for a good five minutes before he showed any signs of life. His mother failed to put in an appearance at all. He said she was sleeping like a baby and hadn't been very well, but according to the officer in charge, no one could have slept through such a disturbance."

"Unless drugged of course," Das said.

"He did find a box of Canbutal capsules on the mantelpiece, which seemed to offer a solution."

"So what you're really wondering is whether or not Mrs. Phillips could have been in bed and asleep when Harold returned home—whenever that was."

"Naturally—I understand Canbutal is pretty powerful stuff. I also understand that it's not usually prescribed in simple cases of insomnia."

Das got to his feet, went to the fireplace and selected a black cheroot from a sandalwood box. "What I tell you now must be treated in the strictest confidence. You're right about Canbutal. It works best in cases where the patient cannot sleep because of extreme pain. It's as close to the old-fashioned knock-out drops as you can get."

"Mrs. Phillips must be pretty ill to need a thing like that."

"Cancer."

There was a moment of silence as if darkness had drifted into the room. Miller took a deep breath and went on, "Does Harold know?"

"She doesn't know herself. She's had bronchial trouble for years. She thinks this is the same thing she gets every winter only a little worse than usual. She'll go very quickly. Any time, any day."

"What kind of an effect would the Canbutal have—can she be awakened, for example?"

"That would depend on the amount taken. Mrs. Phillips is on a dosage of two each night. She visits me once a week and I give her a prescription for a week's supply. As a matter of fact I saw her yesterday morning."

"But she definitely could be awakened even an hour or two after having taken a couple of these things?"

"Certainly. Mind you, it depends on what you mean by awakened. What took place might seem like a dream to her afterwards—there might not even be a memory of it."

Miller got to his feet. "Very helpful—very helpful indeed."

They went out into the hall and Das opened the door for him. "Do you intend to arrest young Phillips? Is there really a case against him?"

"I've been ordered to take him in again for further questioning," Miller said. "I can't be more definite than that. I suppose you've heard that Grant's in hospital after a car accident? That means the Scotland Yard man, Chief Superintendent Mallory, is in charge. If you want to go any further with this, he's the man to see."

"I'm concerned with one thing only," Das said. "The welfare of Mrs. Phillips. I would hope that you could keep the seriousness of this business from her until the last possible moment. If you intend to question her then I think I should be there."

"As I said, I'm going round to pick up her son now," Miller told him. "And there are obviously certain questions I must put to his mother. You're perfectly at liberty to come with me. In fact I'd welcome it."

"Very well," Das said. "I'll follow in my own car. You'll wait for me before entering?"

"Certainly," Miller said and he went down the steps to the Mini-Cooper and drove away.

Brady was standing in the doorway of a newsagent's shop just round the corner from Narcia Street and he ran across the road through the heavy rain and scrambled into the Mini-Cooper as Miller slowed.

"Not bad timing," he said. "I've only just got here." He produced the gloves. "The girl's father recognised these straightaway. He bought them for her as a birthday present. She was with him at the time. He even remembers the shop. That boutique place in Grove Square."

"Good enough," Miller said. "I've seen Das. He tells me you only prescribe Canbutal when a patient can't sleep because of pain."

"So the old girl's in a bad way?"

"You could say that. Das is following on behind,

by the way. He's coming in with us, just in case she gets a funny turn or anything."

"Good enough," Brady said.

A horn sounded behind them as Das arrived. Miller moved into gear, drove round the corner into Narcia Street and pulled up outside number ten.

When Harold opened the door there was a momentary expression of dismay on his face that was replaced in an instant by a brave smile.

"Back again then?" he said to Brady.

"This is Detective Sergeant Miller," Brady said formally. "He'd like a few words with you."

"Oh, yes." Harold glanced at Das curiously. "What are you doing here?"

"I'm interested in one thing only," Das said. "Your mother's welfare. In her present state of health she can't stand shocks so I thought it better to be on hand."

They all went into the living-room and Miller said, "I wonder whether you'd mind getting dressed, sir? We'd like you to come down to Central C.I.D. with us."

"I've already been there once," Harold said. "What is this?"

"Nothing to get excited about, son," Brady said kindly. "One or two new facts have come up about the girl and Chief Superintendent Mallory thinks you might be able to help him, that's all."

"All right then," Harold said. "Give me five minutes."

He went out and Brady picked up the box of Canbutal capsules from the mantelpiece. "These are what she's been taking," he said, holding them out to Miller.

Das took the box, opened it and spilled the capsules out on his palm. He frowned. "I gave her the prescription for these at two-thirty yesterday afternoon. She's taken three since then." He put the capsules back into the box. "I think I'd better go up and see her."

"All right," Miller said. "I'll come with you."

"Is that absolutely necessary?"

Miller nodded. "I must ask her to confirm Harold's story—can't avoid it. Better with you here surely."

"I suppose so. It might help for the present if you could handle it other than as a police enquiry though. Is there really any need to upset her at this stage?"

"I'll do what I can."

Das obviously knew his way. They went up the stairs and he opened the door that stood directly opposite. The curtains were still half-drawn and the room was grey and sombre. The furniture was many years old, mainly heavy Victorian mahogany and the brass bed had now become a collector's item if only its occupant had realised that fact.

She was propped against the pillows, eyes closed,

head turned slightly to one side, the flesh drawn and tight across the bones of her face. Someone on the way out. Miller had seen it before and he knew the signs. Death was a tangible presence, waiting over there in the shadows to take her out of her misery like a good friend.

Das sat on the bed and gently touched her shoulder. "Mrs. Phillips?"

The eyes fluttered open, gazed at him blindly, closed. She took several deep breaths, opened her eyes again and smiled weakly. "Doctor Das."

"How are you today, Mrs. Phillips. Little bit better?"

The Indian's slightly sing-song voice was incredibly soothing carrying with it all the compassion and kindness in the world.

"What day is it, Doctor?" She was obviously muddled and bewildered, the effects of the drug Miller surmised.

"Sunday, my dear. Sunday morning."

She blinked and focussed her eyes on Miller. "Who—who are you?"

Miller came forward and smiled. "I'm a friend of Harold's, Mrs. Phillips. He was supposed to meet me last night, but he didn't turn up. I thought I'd better call and see if everything was all right."

"He's about somewhere," she said in a dead voice.

"A good boy, Harold. He brought me some tea when he came in."

"When would that be, Mrs. Phillips?" Miller said softly.

"When?" She frowned, trying to concentrate. "Last night, I think. That's right—it was last night when he came in." She shook her head. "It gets harder to remember."

"Did Harold tell you that he brought you tea last night, Mrs. Phillips?"

"I don't know—I don't remember. He's a good boy." Her eyes closed. "A good boy."

Behind them the door opened and Harold appeared. "What's going on here?" he demanded angrily.

"Your mother is very ill," Das said. "I must make arrangements to have her admitted to hospital at once." He held up the box of Canbutal capsules. "Did you know she has been increasing her dosage? Didn't I warn you that the effects could be disastrous?"

Harold had turned very pale. Brady appeared behind him and took his arm. "Come on, son," he said. "Let's go."

They moved to the head of the stairs and Miller went after them. "Are those the clothes you were wearing last night?" he asked Harold.

Harold turned, answering in a kind of reflex action, "Sure." Then it dawned on him and fear showed in his eyes. "Here, what is this?"

"Take him down," Miller said and turned away.

Das closed the bedroom door quietly. "Things don't look too good for him, do they?"

"He's in for a bad time, that's as much as I can say at the moment. What about her? Anything I can do?"

"Don't worry. They have a telephone next door. I'll ring for an ambulance and stay with her till it comes. You'll keep me posted?"

Miller nodded and they went downstairs. When he opened the door, rain drifted to meet him, pushed across the slimy cobbles by the wind. He looked down towards the Mini-Cooper where Harold sat in the rear with Brady.

"Sunday morning," he said. "What a hell of a way to make a living."

"We all have a choice, Sergeant," Das told him.

Miller glanced at him sharply, but nothing showed in that brown, enigmatic face. He nodded formally. "I'll be in touch," and moved out into the rain.

14

When they reached Central C.I.D. they took Harold to the Interrogation Room where, in spite of his angry protests, he was relieved of his trousers.

"What the hell do you think you're playing at?" he demanded. "I've got my rights, just like anyone else."

"Our lab boys just want to run a few tests, son, that's all," Brady informed him. "If they come out right, you'll be completely eliminated from the whole enquiry. You'd like that, wouldn't you?"

"You go to hell," Harold shouted furiously. "And you can knock off the Father Christmas act."

There was a knock on the door and a constable entered carrying a pair of police uniform trousers. "Better get into those and do as you're told," Miller said, tossing them across. "You'll make it a lot easier on yourself in the long run." He turned to Brady. "I've got things to do. I'll see you later."

The medical report on Faulkner which C.R.O. had promised was waiting on his desk. He read it through quickly, then again, taking his time. When he was finished, he sat there for a while, staring into space, a frown on his face. He finally got up and crossed to Mallory's office taking the report with him.

The Chief Superintendent was seated at his desk examining a file and glanced up impatiently. "Took you long enough. What's going on then?"

"Brady's got him in the Interrogation Room now, sir. His trousers have gone over to Forensic for examination. I understand Inspector Wade's got one of the Medical School serologists to come in. You should get a quick result."

"You saw the mother?"

Miller told him what had taken place at Narcia Street.

"From the looks of her, I wouldn't give her long."

Mallory nodded. "So Master Harold could have awakened her at any time with that cup of tea, that seems to be what it comes down to. From what the doctor says she wouldn't know whether it was yesterday or today in her condition."

"That's about the size of it."

"Good show." Mallory rubbed his hands together. "I'll let him stew for a while then get to work. I don't think he'll last long."

"You sound pretty certain."

"You're a smart lad, Miller, so I'm going to tell you something for your own good. You don't know what it's all about up here in the sticks. I've been on more murder investigations than you've had hot dinners. You get an instinct for these things, believe me. Harold Phillips killed that girl—I'd stake my reputation on it."

"And what about Faulkner? He's still a strong possibility in my book. Have you read Constable Dwyer's report yet on what happened last night?"

"I know what you're going to say," Mallory said. "He saw Faulkner at a coffee stall in Regent Square just before the murder took place."

"Something he conveniently forgot to mention to us when we questioned him."

"Perfectly understandable in the circumstances."

Miller produced the gloves and tossed them down on the desk. "Those belonged to Grace Packard. Faulkner left them at the coffee stall by mistake."

Mallory picked them up, frowning. "You mean you've been there this morning?"

"That's right. Brady told me about Dwyer's report. I thought I might as well call at the coffee stall on my way to pick young Phillips up, just to see what the proprietor had to say."

"I thought I told you I wanted Phillips picked up right away?" Mallory demanded harshly.

"So I wasted ten minutes. Would it interest you to know that when those gloves dropped out of Faulkner's pocket he told the owner of the coffee stall they belonged to his fiancée? Now why would he do that?"

Mallory laughed in his face. "Because he didn't want him to know he'd been out with another woman or is that too simple for you?"

"But a great many people already knew he'd been in Grace Packard's company that night. Everyone at the party saw him leave with her. Why tell the bloke at the coffee stall such a silly lie at this stage?"

"I think you're placing far too much importance on a very minor incident."

"But is it minor, sir? Inspector Wade reminded us earlier that in every other incident the Rainlover had taken some item or another from the victim. He said that didn't seem to have happened in this case. Can we be certain of that knowing about these gloves?"

"So we're back to the Rainlover again?" Mallory shook his head. "It won't fit, Miller. There are too many other differences."

"All right," Miller said. "But I still think Faulkner has a lot of explaining to do. To start with he was in the girl's company and his reasons for taking her back to the flat were eccentric enough to be highly suspect."

"Not at all," Mallory countered. "Typical behaviour according to his friends and past record."

"He was in the immediate area of the murder only minutes before it took place, we've two witnesses to that. And he lied about the girl's gloves to Harkness."

"Why did he visit the coffee stall? Did Harkness tell you that?"

"To buy cigarettes."

"Was this the first time?"

"No, he frequently appeared at odd hours for the same reason."

"Can you imagine what a good defence counsel would do with that?"

"All right," Miller said. "It's circumstantial—all of it, but there are too many contributing factors to ignore. Take this pattern of violence for example. Unusual in a man of his background. I've got the medical report on him here."

He handed it across and Mallory shook his head. "I haven't got time. Tell me the facts."

"It's simple enough. He was involved in a serious car accident about six years ago—racing at Brand's Hatch. His skull was badly fractured, bone fragments in the brain and so on. He was damned lucky to pull through. His extreme aggressiveness has been a development since then. The psychiatrists who examined him at Wandsworth were definitely of the opinion that the behaviour pattern was a direct result of the brain damage, probably made worse by the fragments of bone which the surgeons had been unable to remove. The pattern of violence grew worse during his sentence. He was involved in several fights with prisoners and attacked a prison officer. He was advised to enter an institution for treatment on his discharge, but refused."

"All right, Miller, all right." Mallory held up both hands defensively. "You go and see him—do anything you like. I'll handle Harold."

"Thank you, sir," Miller said formally.

He got the door half-open and Mallory added,

"One more thing, Miller. A quid says Harold Phillips murdered Grace Packard."

"Fair enough, sir."

"And I'll give you odds of five-to-one against Bruno Faulkner."

"Well, I don't really like to take the money, but if you insist, sir." Miller grinned and gently closed the door.

It was at that precise moment in another part of the city that the man known as the Rainlover opened his Sunday newspaper and found Sean Doyle staring out at him from the middle of page two. He recognised him instantly and sat there staring at the picture for a long moment, remembering the girl standing in the lighted doorway and the darkness and the rain falling.

He had unfinished business there, but first it would be necessary to get rid of the man. Of course he could always telephone the police anonymously, give them the address, tell them that Doyle was in hiding there. On the other hand, they would probably arrest the girl also for harbouring him.

The solution, when it came, was so simple that he

laughed out loud. He was still laughing when he put on his hat and coat and went out into the rain.

Miller got no reply to his persistent knocking at Faulkner's door and finally went down the stairs to the flat below where someone was playing a tenor, cool and clear, so pure that it hurt a little.

The instrumentalist turned out to be an amiable West Indian in dark glasses and a neat fringe beard. He took off the glasses and grinned hugely.

"Aint's I seen you play piano at Chuck Lazer's club?"

"Could be," Miller told him.

"Man, you were the most. Someone told me you was a John." He shook his head. "I tell you, man, you get some real crazy cats around these nights. Sick in the head. They'll say anything. You coming in?"

"I'm looking for Bruno Faulkner. Any idea where he might be? I can't get a reply."

The West Indian chuckled. "Sunday's his brick smashing day."

"Come again?"

"Karate, man. He goes to the Kardon Judo Centre every Sunday morning for a workout. Of course if he can't find any bricks to smash he'd just as soon smash people." He tapped his head. "Nutty as a fruit cake. He don't need the stuff, man. He's already there."

"Thanks for the information," Miller said. "See you sometime."

"The original wild man from Borneo," the West Indian called as he went down the stairs. "That the best you Western European civilisation cats can do? The day is coming, man! The day is coming!"

From the sound of it, he was on the stuff himself, but Miller had other fish to fry and he got into the Mini-Cooper and drove away quickly.

Miller himself had been an ardent student of both judo and karate for several years. A brown belt in both, only the pressure of work had prevented him from progressing further. Although he did most of his own training at the police club, he was familiar with the Kardon Judo Centre and knew Bert King, the senior instructor, well.

There were two dojos and King was in the first supervising free practice with half a dozen young schoolboys. He was a small, shrunken man with a yellowing, parchment-like skin and a head that seemed too large for the rest of him. He was a fourth

Dan in both judo and aikido and incredible in action on the mat as Miller knew to his cost.

King came across, all smiles. "Hello, Sergeant Miller. Not seen you around much lately."

"Never have the time, Bert," Miller said. "I'm looking for a man called Faulkner. Is he here?"

King's smile slipped a little, but he nodded. "Next door."

"You don't think much of him?" Miller demanded, quick to seize any opportunity.

"Too rough for my liking. To tell you the truth he's been on the borderline for getting chucked out of the club for some time now. Forgets himself, that's the trouble. Loses his temper."

"Is he any good?"

"Karate—second Dan and powerful with it. He's good at the showy stuff—smashing bricks, beams of wood and so on. His judo is nowhere. I'll take you in. He's on his own."

Faulkner wore an old judogi which had obviously been washed many times and looked powerful enough as he worked out in front of the full-length mirrors at one end of the dojo, going through the interminable and ritualistic exercises without which no student can hope to attain any standard at all at karate. His kicks were one of his strongest features, very high and fast.

He paused to wipe the sweat from his face with a towel and noticed his audience. He recognised Miller at once and came forward, a sneer on his face.

"Didn't know you allowed coppers in here, Bert, I'll have to reconsider my membership."

"Sergeant Miller's welcome here any time," King said, his face flushed with anger. "And I'd be careful about going on the mat with him if I were you. You could get a nasty surprise."

Which was a slight exaggeration judging from what Miller had just seen, but Faulkner chuckled softly. "And now you're tempting me—you really are."

King went out and Faulkner rubbed his head briskly. "I'm beginning to get you for breakfast, dinner and tea. Rather boring."

"I can't help that," Miller said and produced Grace Packard's gloves from his pocket. "Recognise these?"

Faulkner examined then and sighed. "Don't tell me. I left them at Sam Harkness's coffee stall in Regent Square last night. As I remember, I pulled them out of my pocket when looking for some loose change. He said something about them not being my style."

"And you told him they belonged to your fiancée."

"I know, Miller, very naughty of me. They were the Packard girl's. She left them at the flat."

"Why did you lie about it to Harkness?"

"Be your age—why should I discuss my private affairs with him?"

"You've never seemed to show that kind of reluctance before."

Faulkner's face went dark. "Anything else, because if not I'd like to get on with my work-out?"

"You've had that. You've got a lot of explaining to do, Faulkner. A hell of a lot."

"I see. Am I going to be arrested?"

"That remains to be seen."

"So I'm still a free agent?" He glanced at his watch. "I'll be here for another twenty minutes, Miller. After that I'll shower for five minutes, dress and take a taxi to my flat. If I have to see you, I'll see you there and nowhere else. Now good morning to you."

He turned and stalked across the mat to the mirrors, positioned himself and started to practice front kicks. Strangely enough Miller didn't feel angry at all. In any case the flat would be preferable to the judo centre for the kind of conversation he envisaged. The important thing was that there was something there, something to be brought into the light. He was certain of that now. He turned and went out quickly, his stomach hollow with excitement.

15

The Gunner came awake slowly, yawned and stretched his arms. For a moment he stared blankly around him, wondering where he was and then he remembered.

It was quiet there in the comfortable old living-room—so quiet that he could hear the clock ticking and the soft patter of the rain as it drifted against the window.

The blanket with which Jenny Crowther had covered him had slipped down to his knees. He touched it gently for a moment, a smile on his mouth, then got to his feet and stretched again. The fire was almost out. He dropped to one knee, raked the ashes away and added a little of the kindling he found in the coal scuttle. He waited until the flames were dancing and then went into the kitchen.

He filled the kettle, lit the gas stove and helped himself to a cigarette from a packet he found on the table. He went to the window and peered out into the rain-swept yard and behind him, Jenny Crowther said, "Never stops, does it?"

She wore an old bathrobe and the black hair hung straight on either side of a face that was clear and shining and without a line.

"No need to ask you if you slept well," he said. "You look as if they've just turned you out at the mint."

She smiled right down to her toes and crossed to the window, yawning slightly. "As a matter of fact I slept better than I have done for weeks. I can't understand it."

"That's because I was here, darlin'," he quipped. "Guarding the door like some faithful old hound."

"There could be something in that," she said soberly.

There was an awkward pause. It was as if neither of them could think of the right thing to say next, as if out of some inner knowledge they both knew that they had walked a little further towards the edge of some quiet place where anything might happen.

She swilled out the teapot and reached for the caddy and the Gunner chuckled. "Sunday morning— used to be my favourite day of the week. You could smell the bacon frying all the way up to the bedroom."

"Who was doing the cooking?"

"My Aunt Mary of course." He tried to look hurt. "What kind of a bloke do you think I am? The sort that keeps stray birds around the place?"

"I'm glad you put that in the plural. Very honest of you."

On impulse, he moved in behind her and slid his arms about her waist, pulling her softness against him, aware from the feel of her that beneath the bathrobe she very probably had nothing on.

"Two and a half bleeding years in the nick. I've forgotten what it's like."

"Well, you needn't think you're going to take it out on me."

She turned to glance over her shoulder, smiling and then the smile faded and she turned completely, putting a hand up to his face.

"Oh, Gunner, you're a daft devil, aren't you?"

His hands cupped her rear lightly and he dropped

his head until his forehead rested against hers. For some reason he felt like crying, all choked up so that he couldn't speak, just like being a kid again, uncertain in a cold world.

"Don't rub it in, lass."

She tilted his chin and kissed him very gently on the mouth. He pushed her away firmly and held her off, a hand on each shoulder. What he said next surprised even himself.

"None of that now. You don't want to be mixed up with a bloke like me. Nothing but a load of trouble. I'll have a cup of tea and something to eat and then I'll be off. You and the old girl had better forget you ever saw me."

"Why don't you shut up?" she said. "Go and sit down by the fire and I'll bring the tea in."

He sat in the easy chair and watched her arrange the tray with a woman's instinctive neatness and pour tea into two cups. "What about the old girl?"

"She'll be hard on till noon," Jenny said. "Needs plenty of rest at her age."

He sat there drinking his tea, staring into the fire and she said softly, "What would you do then if this was an ordinary Sunday?"

"In the nick?" He chuckled grimly. "Oh, you get quite a choice. You can go to the services in the prison chapel morning and evening—plenty of the lads do that, just to get out of their cells. Otherwise you're locked in all day."

"What do you do?"

"Read, think. If you're in a cell with someone else you can always play chess, things like that. If you're at the right stage in your sentence they let you out on to the landing for an hour or so in the evening to play table tennis or watch television."

She shook her head. "What a waste."

He grinned and said with a return to his old flippancy, "Oh, I don't know. What would I be doing Sundays on the outside? Spend the morning in the kip. Get up for three or four pints at the local and back in time for roast beef, Yorkshire pud and two veg. I'd have a snooze after that, work me way through the papers in the afternoon and watch the telly in the evening. What a bloody bore."

"Depends who you're doing it with," she suggested.

"You've got a point there. Could put an entirely different complexion on the morning in the kip for a start."

She put down her cup and leaned forward. "Why not go back, Gunner? There's nowhere to run to. The longer you leave it, the worse it will be."

"I could lose all my remission," he said. "That would mean another two and a half years."

"Are you certain you'd lose all of it?"

"I don't know. You have to take your chance on that sort of thing." He grinned. "Could have been back now if things had turned out differently last night."

"What do you mean?" He told her about Doreen and what had happened at her flat. When he finished, Jenny shook her head. "What am I going to do with you?"

"I could make a suggestion. Two and a half years is a hell of a long time."

She examined him critically and frowned. "You know I hadn't realised it before, but you could do with a damned good scrub. You'll find a bathroom at the head of the stairs and there's plenty of hot water. Go on. I'll make you some breakfast while you're in the tub."

"All right then, all right," he said good-humouredly as she pulled him to his feet and pushed him through the door.

But he wasn't smiling when he went upstairs and locked himself in the bathroom. *Two and a half years*. The thought of it sent a wave of coldness through him, of sudden, abject despair. If only that stupid screw hadn't decided to sneak off to the canteen. If only he hadn't tried to touch up the staff nurse. But that was the trouble with life, wasn't it? Just one big series of ifs.

He was just finishing dressing when she knocked on the door and said softly, "Come into my room when you've finished, Gunner—it's the next door. I've got some clean clothes for you."

When he went into her room she was standing at the end of the bed bending over a suit which she had laid out. "My father's," she said. "Just about the right fit I should say."

"I can't take that, darlin'," the Gunner told her. "If the coppers catch me in gear like that they'll want to know where it came from."

She stared at him, wide-eyed. "I hadn't thought of that."

"If I go back it's got to be just the way I looked when I turned up here last night otherwise they'll want to know where I've been and who's been helping me."

The room was strangely familiar and he looked around him and grinned. "You want to get a curtain for that window, darlin'. When I was in the loft last night I could see right in. Quite a view. One I'm not likely to forget in a hurry." He sighed and said in a whisper, "I wonder how many times I'll think of that during the next two and a half years."

"Look at me, Gunner," she said softly.

When he turned she was standing at the end of the bed. She was quite naked, her bathrobe on the floor at her feet. The Gunner was turned to stone. She was so lovely it hurt. She just stood there looking at him calmly, waiting for him to make a move, the hair like a dark curtain sweeping down until it gently brushed against the tips of the firm breasts.

He went towards her slowly, reaching out to touch like a blind man. Her perfume filled his nostrils and a kind of hoarse sob welled up in his throat.

He held her tightly in his arms, his head buried against her shoulder and she smoothed his hair and kissed him gently as a mother might a child. "It's all right, Gunner. Everything's going to be all right."

Gunner Doyle, the great lover. He was like some kid presented with the real thing for the first time. His hands were shaking so much that she had to unbutton his shirt and trousers for him. But afterwards it was fine, better than he had ever known it before. He melted into her flesh as she pulled him close and carried him away into warm, aching darkness.

* * *

Afterwards—a long time afterwards, or so it seemed—the telephone started to ring. "I'd better see who it is." She slipped from beneath the sheets, and reached for her bathrobe.

The door closed softly behind her and the Gunner got up and started to dress. He was fastening his belt when the door opened again and she stood there staring at him looking white and for the first time since he had known her, frightened.

He took her by the shoulders. "What's up?"

"It was a man," she said in a strained voice. "A man on the phone. He said to tell you to get out fast. That the police would be here any time."

"Jesus," he said. "Who was it?"

"I don't know," she said and cracked suddenly. "Oh, Gunner, what are we going to do?"

"You stay put, darlin', and carry on as normal," he said, going to the bed and pulling on the boots she had given him. "I'm the only one who has to do anything."

He yanked the sweater over his head and she grabbed his arm. "Give yourself up, Gunner."

"First things first, darlin'. I've got to get out of here and so far away that the coppers don't have a hope of connecting me with you and the old girl."

She looked up into his face for a moment then turned to the dressing-table and opened her handbag.

She took out a handful of loose coins and three pound notes.

When she held the money out to him he tried to protest, but she shook her head. "Better take it, just in case you decide to keep on running. I'm not holding you to anything." She went to the wardrobe and produced an old single-breasted raincoat. "And this. It was my father's. No use to him now."

Suddenly she was the tough Yorkshire lass again, rough, competent, completely unsentimental. "Now you'd better get out of here."

He pulled on the coat and she led the way into the passageway. The Gunner started towards the stairs and she jerked his sleeve. "I've got a better way."

He followed her up another flight of stairs, passing several doors which obviously led to upper rooms. At the top, they were confronted by a heavier door bolted on the inside and protected by a sheet of iron against burglars.

She eased back the bolts and the door swung open in the wind giving him a view of a flat roof between two high gables. There was a rail at one end and on the other side of it the roof sloped to the yard below.

"If you scramble over the gable end," she said, pointing to the left, "you can slide down the other side to the flat roof of a metalworks next door. Nothing to it for you—I've done it myself when I was a kid. You'll find a fire escape that'll take you all the way down into the next alley."

He stared at her dumbly, rain blowing in through the open doorway, unable to think of anything to say. She gave him a sudden fierce push that sent him out into the open.

"Go on—get moving, you bloody fool," she said and slammed the door.

He had never felt so utterly desolate, so completely cut-off from everything in his life. It was as if he had left everything worth having back there behind that iron door and there was nothing he could do about it. Not a damned thing.

He followed her instructions to the letter and a minute or so later hurried along the alley on the far side and turned into the street at the end.

He kept on walking in a kind of daze, his mind elsewhere, turning from one street into the other in the heavy rain. About ten minutes later he found himself on the edge of Jubilee Park. He went in through a corner entrance, past the enigmatic statue of good Queen Victoria, orb in one hand and sceptre in the other, and walked aimlessly into the heart of the park.

He didn't see a living soul which was hardly surprising considering the weather. Finally he came to an old folks' pavilion, the kind of place where pensioners congregated on calmer days to gossip and play dominos. The door was locked, but a bench beside it was partially sheltered from the rain by an overhanging roof. He slumped down, hands thrust deep into the pockets of the old raincoat and stared into the grey curtain. He was alone in a dead world. Completely and finally alone.

16

When Faulkner got out of the taxi there was no sign of Nick Miller. Faulkner was surprised, but hardly in a mood to shed tears over the matter. He hurried up to his flat, unlocked the door and went in. The fire had almost gone out and he took off his wet raincoat, got down on one knee and started to replenish it carefully. As the flames started to flicker into life the door bell sounded.

He opened it, expecting Miller, and found Joanna and Jack Morgan standing there.

"Surprise, surprise," Faulkner said.

"Cut it out, Bruno," Morgan told him. "We had a

visit from Nick Miller early this morning and what he told us wasn't funny."

Faulkner took Joanna's coat. "This whole thing is beginning to annoy me and there's a nasty hint of worse to come. Visions of a lonely cell with two hard-faced screws, the parson snivelling at my side as I take that last walk along the corridor to the execution room."

"You should read the papers more often. They aren't hanging murderers this season."

"What a shame. No romance in anything these days, is there?"

Joanna pulled him round to face her. "Can't you be serious for once? You're in real trouble. What on earth possessed you to bring that girl back here?"

"So you know about that, do you?"

"Miller told us, but I'd still like to hear about it from you," Morgan said. "After all, I am your lawyer."

"And that's a damned sinister way of putting it for a start."

The door bell rang sharply. In the silence that followed, Faulkner grinned. "Someone I've been expecting. Excuse me a moment."

* * *

When Miller left the judo centre he was feeling strangely elated. At the best of times police work is eighty per cent instinct—a special faculty that comes from years of handling every kind of trouble. In this present case his intuition told him that Faulkner had something to hide, whatever Mallory's opinion might be. The real difficulty was going to be in digging it out.

He sat in the car for a while, smoking a cigarette and thinking about it. Faulkner was a highly intelligent man and something of a natural actor. He enjoyed putting on a show and being at the centre of things. His weakness obviously lay in his disposition to sudden, irrational violence, to a complete emotional turnabout during which he lost all control or at least that's what his past history seemed to indicate. If only he could be pushed over the edge . . .

Miller was filled with a kind of restless excitement at the prospect of the encounter to come and that was no good at all. He parked the car beside the corner gate of Jubilee Park, buttoned his trenchcoat up to the chin and went for a walk.

He didn't mind the heavy rain—rather liked it, in fact. It somehow seemed to hold him safe in a small private world in which he was free to think without distraction. He walked aimlessly for twenty minutes or so, turning from one path to another, not really seeing very much, his mind concentrated on one thing.

If he had been a little more alert he would have noticed the figure of a man disappearing fast round the side of the old folks' shelter as he approached, but he didn't and the Gunner watched him go, heart in mouth, from behind a rhododendron bush.

When Miller walked in to the flat and found Joanna Hartmann and Morgan standing by the fire he wasn't in the least put out for their presence suited him very well indeed.

He smiled and nodded to the woman as he unbuttoned his damp raincoat. "We seem to have seen rather a lot of each other during the past twenty-four hours."

"Is there any reason why I shouldn't be here?" she demanded coldly.

"Good heavens no. I've just got one or two loose ends to tie up with Mr. Faulkner. Shouldn't take more than five minutes."

"I understand you've already asked him a great many questions," Morgan said, "and now you intend to ask some more. I think we have a right to know where we stand in this matter."

"Are you asking me as his legal representative?"

"Naturally."

"Quite unnecessary, I assure you." Miller lied smoothly. "I'm simply asking him to help me with my enquiries, that's all. He isn't the only one involved."

"I'm happy to hear it."

"Shut up, Jack, there's a good chap," Faulkner cut in. "If you've anything to say to me, then get on with it, Miller. The sooner this damned thing is cleared up, the sooner I can get back to work."

"Fair enough." Miller moved towards the statues. "In a way we have a parallel problem. I understand you started five weeks ago with one figure. In a manner of speaking, so did I."

"A major difference if I might point it out," Faulkner said. "You now have five while I only have four."

"But you were thinking of adding a fifth, weren't you?"

"Which is why I paid Grace Packard to pose for me, but it didn't work." Faulkner shook his head. "No, the damned thing is going to be cast as you see it now for good or ill."

"I see." Miller turned from the statues briskly. "One or two more questions if you don't mind. Perhaps you'd rather I put them to you in private."

"I've nothing to hide."

"As you like. I'd just like to go over things again briefly. Mr. Morgan called for you about eight?"

"That's right."

"What were you doing?"

"Sleeping. I'd worked non-stop on the fourth figure in the group for something like thirty hours. When it was finished I took the telephone off the hook and lay on the bed."

"And you were awakened by Mr. Morgan?"

"That's it."

"And then went to The King's Arms where you met Grace Packard? You're quite positive you hadn't met her previously?"

"What are you trying to suggest?" Joanna interrupted angrily.

"You don't need to answer that, Bruno," Morgan said.

"What in the hell are you both trying to do . . . hang me? Why shouldn't I answer it? I've got nothing to hide. I should think Harry Meadows, the landlord, would be the best proof of that. As I recall, I had to ask him who she was. If you must know I thought she was on the game. I wasn't looking forward to the party and I thought she might liven things up."

"And you met her boy friend on the way out?"

"That's it. He took a swing at me so I had to put him on his back."

"Rather neatly according to the landlord. What did you use . . . judo?"

"Aikido."

"I understand there was also some trouble at the party with Mr. Marlowe?"

Faulkner shrugged. "I wouldn't have called it trouble exactly. Frank isn't the physical type."

"But you are—or so it would seem?"

"What are you trying to prove?" Joanna demanded, moving to Faulkner's side.

"Just trying to get at the facts," Miller said.

Morgan moved forward a step. "I'd say you were aiming at rather more than that. You don't have to put up with this, Bruno."

"Oh, but I do." Faulkner grinned. "It's beginning to get rather interesting. All right, Miller, I've an uncontrollable temper, I'm egotistical, aggressive and when people annoy me I tend to hit them. They even sent me to prison for it once. Common assault—the respectable kind, by the way, not the nasty sexual variety."

"I'm aware of that."

"Somehow I thought you might be."

"You brought the girl back here to pose for you and nothing else?"

"You know when she got here, you know when she left. There wasn't time for anything else."

"Can you remember what you talked about?"

"There wasn't much time for conversation either. I told her to strip and get up on the platform. Then I saw to the fire and poured myself a drink. As soon as she got up there I knew it was no good. I told her to get dressed and gave her a ten-pound note."

"There was no sign of it in her handbag."

"She slipped it into her stocking top. Made a crack about it being the safest place."

"It was nowhere on her person and she's been examined thoroughly."

"All right, so the murderer took it."

Miller decided to keep the information that the girl had had intercourse just before her death to himself for a moment. "There was no question of any sexual assault so how would the murderer have known where it was?"

There was a heavy silence. He allowed it to hang there for a moment and continued, "You're quite sure that you and the girl didn't have an argument before she left?"

Faulkner laughed harshly. "If you mean did I blow my top, break her neck with one devastating karate chop and carry her down the back stairs into the night because she refused my wicked way with her, no. If I'd wanted her to stay the night she'd have stayed and not for any ten quid either. She came cheaper than that or I miss my guess."

"I understand she was found in Dob Court, Sergeant?" Morgan said.

"That's right."

"And are you seriously suggesting that Mr. Faulkner killed the girl here, carted her downstairs and carried her all the way because that's what he would have to have done. I think I should point out that he doesn't own a car."

"They took my licence away last year," Faulkner admitted amiably. "Driving under the influence."

"But you did go out after the girl left?"

"To the coffee stall in Regent Square." Faulkner made no attempt to deny it. "I even said hello to the local bobby. I often do. No class barriers for me."

"He's already told us that. It was only five or ten minutes later that he found Grace Packard's body.

You left Joanna's gloves on the counter. The proprietor asked me to pass them on."

Miller produced the black and white gloves and handed them to Joanna Hartmann who frowned in puzzlement. "But these aren't mine."

"They're Grace Packard's," Faulkner said. "I pulled them out of my pocket when I was looking for some change, as you very well know, Miller. I must have left them on the counter."

"The man at the coffee stall confirms that. Only one difference. Apparently when he commented on them, you said they belonged to Joanna."

Joanna Hartmann looked shocked, but Faulkner seemed quite unperturbed. "He knows Joanna well. We've been there together often. I'd hardly be likely to tell him they belonged to another woman, would I? As I told you earlier, it was none of his business, anyway."

"That seems reasonable enough surely," Joanna said.

Miller looked at her gravely. "Does it?"

She seemed genuinely puzzled. "I don't understand. What are you trying to say?"

Morgan had been listening to everything, a frown of concentration on his face and now he said quickly,

"Just a minute. There's something more here, isn't there?"

"There could be."

For the first time Faulkner seemed to have had enough. The urbane mask slipped heavily and he said sharply, "I'm beginning to get rather bored with all this. Is this or is it not another Rainlover murder?"

Miller didn't even hesitate. "It certainly has all the hallmarks."

"Then that settles it," Morgan said. "You surely can't be suggesting that Mr. Faulkner killed the other four as well?"

"I couldn't have done the previous one for a start," Faulkner said. "I just wasn't available."

"Can you prove that?"

"Easily. There were three statues up there two days ago. Now there are four. Believe me, I was occupied. When Jack called for me last night I hadn't been out of the flat since Thursday."

"You still haven't answered my question, Sergeant," Morgan said. "The gloves . . . you were getting at something else, weren't you?"

"In killings of this kind there are always certain details not released to the Press," Miller said. "Sometimes because they are too unpleasant, but more often because public knowledge of them might prejudice police enquiries."

He was on a course now which might well lead to disaster, he knew that, and if anything went wrong there would be no one to help him, no one to back him up. Mallory would be the first to reach for the axe, but he had gone too far to draw back now.

"This type of compulsive killer is a prisoner of his own sickness. He not only has the compulsion to kill again. He can no more alter his method than stop breathing and that's what always proves his undoing."

"Fascinating," Faulkner said. "Let's see now, Jack the Ripper always chose a prostitute and performed a surgical operation. The Boston Strangler raped them first then choked them with a nylon stocking. What about the Rainlover?"

"No pattern where the women themselves are concerned. The eldest was fifty and Grace Packard was the youngest. No sexual assault, no perversions. Everything neat and tidy. Always the neck broken cleanly from the rear. A man who knows what he's doing."

"Sorry to disappoint you, but you don't need to be a karate expert to break a woman's neck from the rear. One good rabbit punch is all it takes."

"Possibly, but the Rainlover has one other trademark. He always takes something personal from his victims."

"A kind of *memento mori*? Now that is interesting."

"Anything special?" Morgan asked.

"In the first case it was a handbag, then a head-scarf, a nylon stocking and a shoe."

"And in Grace Packard's case a pair of gloves?" Faulkner suggested. "Then tell me this, Miller? If I was content with one shoe and one stocking previously why should it suddenly be necessary for me to take two gloves? A break in the pattern, surely?"

"A good point," Miller admitted.

"Here's another," Joanna said. "What about the ten-pound note? Doesn't that make two items missing?"

"I'm afraid we only have Mr. Faulkner's word that it existed at all."

There was a heavy silence. For the first time Faulkner looked serious—really serious. Morgan couldn't think of anything to say and Joanna Hartmann was just plain frightened.

Miller saw it as the psychological moment to withdraw for a little while and smiled pleasantly. "I'd better get in touch with Headquarters, just to see how things are getting on at that end."

Faulkner tried to look nonchalant and waved towards the telephone. "Help yourself."

"That's all right. I can use the car radio. I'll be back in five minutes. I'm sure you could all use the break."

He went out quickly, closing the door softly behind him.

Faulkner was the first to break the silence with a short laugh that echoed back to him, hollow and strained. "Well, now, it doesn't look too good, does it?"

17

Harold Phillips was hot and uncomfortable. The Interrogation Room was full of cigarette smoke and it was beginning to make his eyes hurt. He'd already had one lengthy session with Chief Superintendent Mallory and he hadn't liked it. He glanced furtively across the room at the stony-faced constable standing beside the door.

He moistened his lips. "How much longer then?"

"That's up to Mr. Mallory, sir," the constable replied.

The door opened and Mallory returned, Brady following him. "Did they get you a cup of tea?" the Superintendent asked.

"No, they didn't," Harold answered in an aggrieved tone.

"That's not good enough—not good enough at all." He turned to the constable. "Fetch a cup of tea from the canteen on the double for Mr. Phillips."

He turned, smiling amiably and sat at the table. He opened a file and glanced at it quickly as he started to fill his pipe. "Let's just look at this again."

In the silence which followed the only sound was the clock ticking on the wall and the dull rumble of thunder somewhere far off in the distance.

"Sounds like more rain then," Harold commented.

Mallory looked up. His face was like stone, the eyes dark and full of menace. He said sharply and angrily, "I'm afraid you haven't been telling the truth, young man. You've been wasting my time."

The contrast between this and his earlier politeness was quite shattering and Harold started to shake involuntarily. "I don't know what you mean," he stammered. "I've told you everything I can remember."

"Tell him the truth, son," Brady put in, worried and anxious. "It'll go better with you in the long run."

"But I am telling him the bleeding truth," Harold cried. "What else does he want—blood? Here, I'm not having any more of this. I want to see a lawyer."

"Lie number one," Mallory said remorselessly. "You told us that you didn't know the name of the man you'd had the argument with at The King's Arms. The man who went off with Grace Packard."

"That's right."

"The landlord remembers differently. He says that when you came back to the pub to take him up on his offer of a drink on the house, you already knew the name of the person concerned. What you'd really come back for was his address only the landlord wouldn't play."

"It's a lie," Harold said. "There isn't a word of truth in it."

"He's ready to repeat his statement under oath in the box," Brady said.

Mallory carried on as if he hadn't heard. "You told us that you were home by half-nine, that you took your mother a cup of tea and then went to bed. Do you still stick to that story?"

"You ask her—she'll tell you. Go on, just ask her."

"We happen to know that your mother is a very sick woman and in severe pain most of the time. The pills the doctor gave to make her sleep needed to be much stronger than usual. Her dosage was two. We can prove she took three yesterday. Medical evidence would indicate that it would be most unlikely that you would have been able to waken her at the time you state."

"You can't prove that." Harold sounded genuinely indignant.

"Possibly not," Mallory admitted candidly, "but it won't look good, will it?"

"So what. You need evidence in a court of law—real evidence. Everybody knows that."

"Oh, we can supply some of that as well if you insist. You told us that after leaving The King's Arms you didn't see Grace Packard again, that you walked round the streets for a while, had a coffee at the station buffet and went home, arriving at half-nine."

"That's right."

"But you found time for something else, didn't you?"

"What are you talking about?"

"You had intercourse with someone."

Harold was momentarily stunned. When he spoke again he was obviously badly shaken. "I don't know what you mean."

"I wouldn't try lying again if I were you. You asked for evidence, real evidence. I've got some for you. For the past couple of hours your trousers, the trousers you were wearing yesterday have been the subject of chemical tests in our laboratory. They haven't finished yet by any means, but I've just had a preliminary report that indicates beyond any shadow of a doubt that you were with a woman last night."

"Maybe someone forgot to tell you, son," Brady put in, "but Grace Packard had intercourse just before she died."

"Here, you needn't try that one." Harold put out a hand defensively. "All right, I'll tell you the truth. I did go with a woman last night."

"Who was she?" Mallory asked calmly.

"I don't know. I bumped into her in one of those streets behind the station."

"Was she on the game?" Brady suggested.

"That's it. Thirty bob for a short time. You know how it goes. We stood against the wall in a back alley."

"And her name?" Mallory said.

"Do me a favour, Superintendent. I didn't even get a clear look at her face."

"Let's hope she hasn't left you something to remember her by," Brady said grimly. "Why didn't you tell us about this before?"

Harold had obviously recovered some of his lost confidence. He contrived to look pious. "It isn't the sort of thing you like to talk about, now is it?"

The constable came in with a cup of tea, placed it

on the table and whispered in Mallory's ear. The Chief Superintendent nodded, got to his feet and beckoned to Brady.

"Miller's on the phone," he said when they got into the corridor.

"What about Harold, sir?"

"Let him stew for a few minutes."

He spoke to Miller from a booth half-way along the corridor. "Where are you speaking from?"

"Phone box outside Faulkner's place," Miller told him. "He's up there now with his lawyer and Joanna Hartmann."

"You've spoken to him then?"

"Oh, yes, thought I'd give him a breather, that's all. We've reached an interesting stage. You were right about the gloves, sir. He didn't even attempt to deny having had them. Gave exactly the reason for lying about them at the coffee stall that you said he would."

Mallory couldn't help feeling slightly complacent. "There you are then. I don't like to say I told you so, but I honestly think you're wasting your time, Miller."

"Don't tell me Harold's cracked?"

"Not quite, but he's tying himself up in about

fifty-seven different knots. I think he's our man. More certain of it than ever."

"But not the Rainlover?"

"A different problem, I'm afraid."

"One interesting point, sir," Miller said. "Remember Faulkner told us he gave the girl ten pounds?"

"What about it?"

"What he actually gave her was a ten-pound note. He says she tucked it into her stocking top. Apparently made some crack about it being the safest place."

"Now that is interesting." Mallory was aware of a sudden tightness in his chest that interfered with his breathing—an old and infallible sign. "That might just about clinch things if I use it in the right way. I think you'd better get back here right away, Miller."

"But what about Faulkner, sir?"

"Oh, to hell with Faulkner, man. Get back here now and that's an order."

He slammed down the phone and turned to Brady who waited, leaning against the wall. "Miller's just come up with an interesting tit-bit. Remember Faulkner said he gave the girl ten pounds for posing for him. He's just told Miller it was actually a ten-pound note. Now I wonder what our friend in there would do with it."

"Always assuming that he's the man we want, sir," Brady reminded him.

"Now don't you start, Brady," Mallory said. "I've got enough on my hands with Miller."

"All right, sir," Brady said. "Put a match to it if he had any sense."

"Which I doubt," Mallory chuckled grimly. "Can you imagine Harold Phillips putting a match to a ten-pound note?" He shook his head. "Not on your life. He'll have stashed it away somewhere."

At that moment Henry Wade appeared from the lift at the end of the corridor and came towards them, Harold's trousers over his arm.

"Anything else for me?" Mallory demanded.

Wade shook his head. "I'm afraid not. He was with a woman, that's all I can tell you."

"Nothing more?"

Wade shrugged. "No stains we can link with the girl if that's what you mean. Sometimes if you're lucky you can test the semen for its blood group factor. About forty per cent of males secrete their blood group in their body fluids. Of course it won't work if the subject isn't a member of that group. In any case you need a large specimen and it's got to be fresh. Sorry, sir."

Mallory took a deep breath. "All right, this is what

we do. We're all going back in there. I want you to simply stand with the trousers over your arm and say nothing, Wade. Brady—just look serious. That's all I ask."

"But what are you going to try, sir?" Brady demanded.

"A king-size bluff," Mallory said simply. "I'm simply betting on the fact that I'm a better poker player than Harold Phillips."

18

Nick Miller replaced the receiver and stepped out of the telephone box into the heavy rain. Mallory's instructions had been quite explicit. He was to drop the Faulkner enquiry and return to Headquarters at once and yet the Scotland Yard man was wrong—Miller still felt certain about that. It was nothing he could really put his finger on, something that couldn't be defined and yet when he thought of Faulkner his stomach went hollow and his flesh crawled.

But orders were orders and to disobey this one was to invite the kind of reaction that might mean the end of his career as a policeman. When it finally came down to it he wasn't prepared to throw away a life that had come to mean everything to him simply because of a private hunch that could well be wrong.

He crossed to the Mini-Cooper, took out his keys and, above his head, the studio window of Faulkner's flat dissolved in a snowstorm of flying glass as a chair soared through in a graceful curve that ended in the middle of the street.

There was a heavy silence after Miller left and Faulkner was the first to break it. He crossed to the bar and poured himself a large gin. "I can feel the noose tightening already. Distinctly unpleasant."

"Stop it, Bruno!" Joanna said sharply. "It just isn't funny any more."

He paused, the glass half-way to his lips and looked at her in a kind of mild surprise. "You surely aren't taking this thing seriously?"

"How else can I take it?"

Faulkner turned his attention to Morgan. "And what about you?"

"It doesn't look too good, Bruno."

"That's wonderful. That's bloody marvellous." Faulkner drained his glass and came round from behind the bar. "How long have you known me, Jack?

Fifteen years or is it more? I'd be fascinated to know when you first suspected my homicidal tendencies."

"Why did you have to bring that wretched girl back with you, Bruno? Why?" Joanna said.

He looked at them both in turn, his cynical smile fading. "My God, you're both beginning to believe it, aren't you? You're actually beginning to believe it."

"Don't be ridiculous." Joanna turned away.

He swung her round to face him. "No, you're afraid to give it voice, but it's there in your eyes."

"Please, Bruno . . . you're hurting me."

He pushed her away and turned on Jack. "And you?"

"You've a hell of a temper, Bruno, no one knows that better than I do. When you broke Pearson's jaw it took four of us to drag you off him."

"Thanks for the vote of confidence."

"Face facts, Bruno. Miller's got a lot to go on. All circumstantial, I'll grant you that, but it wouldn't look good in court."

"That's your opinion."

"All right, let's look at the facts as the prosecution would present them to a jury. First of all there's your uncontrollable temper, your convictions for violence. The medical report when you were in Wandsworth said you needed psychiatric treatment, but you refused. That won't look good for a start."

"Go on—this is fascinating."

"You bring Grace Packard back here late at night and give her ten pounds to pose for you for two or three minutes."

"The simple truth."

"I know that—I believe it because it's typical of you, but if you think there's a jury in England that would swallow such an explanation you're crazy."

"You're not leaving me with much hope, are you?"

"I'm not finished yet." Morgan carried on relentlessly. "No more than a couple of minutes after she left you went out after her. You bought cigarettes at that coffee stall in Regent Square and she was killed not more than two hundred yards away a few minutes later. And you had her gloves—can you imagine what the prosecution would try to make out of that one?"

Faulkner seemed surprisingly calm considering the circumstances. "And what about the ten-pound note? If it didn't exist why should I bother to mention it in the first place?"

"A further complication . . . all part of the smoke-screen."

"And you believe that?"

"I think a jury might."

Faulkner went to the bar, reached for the gin bottle and poured himself another drink. He stood with his back to them for a moment. When he finally turned, he looked calm and serious.

"A good case, Jack, but one or two rather obvious flaws. You've laid some stress on the fact that I had Grace Packard's gloves. I think it's worth pointing out that I had them before she was killed. In any case, the gloves are only important if you maintain that Grace Packard was killed by the Rainlover. Have you considered that?"

"Yes, I've considered it," Morgan said gravely.

"But if I am the Rainlover then I killed the others and you'd have to prove that was possible. What about the woman killed the night before last for example? As I told you when you called for me last night, I'd been working two days non-stop. Hadn't even left the studio."

"The body was found in Jubilee Park no more than a quarter of a mile from here. You could have left by the back stairs and returned inside an hour and no one the wiser. That's what the prosecution would say."

"But I didn't know about the murder, did I? You had to tell me. Don't you remember? It was just after you arrived. I was dressing in the bedroom and you spoke to me from in here."

Morgan nodded. "That's true. I remember now. I asked if you'd heard about the killing, picked up the paper and discovered it was Friday night's." He seemed to go rigid and added in a whisper, "Friday night's."

He went to the chair by the fire, picked up the newspaper that was still lying there as it had been on his arrival the previous evening. "Final edition, Friday 23rd." He turned to Faulkner. "But you don't have a paper delivered."

"So what?"

"Then how did you get hold of this if you didn't leave the house for two days?"

Joanna gave a horrified gasp and for the first time Faulkner really looked put out. He put a hand to his head, frowning. "I remember now. I ran out of cigarettes. I was tired . . . so tired that I couldn't think straight and it was raining hard, beating against the window." It was almost as if he was speaking to himself. "I thought the air might clear my head and I needed some cigarettes so I slipped out."

"And the newspaper?"

"I got it from the old man on the corner of Albany Street."

"Next to Jubilee Park."

They stood there in tableau, the three of them, caught in a web of silence and somewhere in the distance thunder echoed menacingly. Morgan was white and strained and a kind of horror showed in Joanna's face.

Faulkner shook his head slowly as if unable to comprehend what was happening. "You must believe me, Joanna, you must."

She turned to Morgan. "Take me home, Jack. Please take me home."

Faulkner said angrily, "I'll be damned if I'll let you go like this."

As he grabbed at her arm she moved away sharply, colliding with the drawing board on its stand, the one at which Faulkner had been working earlier. The board went over, papers scattering and his latest sketch fell at her feet, a rough drawing of the group of four statues with a fifth added.

There was real horror on her face at this final, terrible proof. As she backed away, Morgan picked up the sketch and held it out to Faulkner. "Have you got an explanation for this, too?"

Faulkner brushed him aside and grabbed Joanna by both arms. "Listen to me—just listen. That's all I ask."

She slapped at him in a kind of blind panic and Morgan tried to pull Faulkner away from her. Something snapped inside Faulkner. He turned and hit

Morgan back-handed, sending him staggering against the bar.

Joanna ran for the door. Faulkner caught her before she could open it and wrenched her around, clutching at the collar of her sheepskin coat.

"You're not leaving me, do you hear? I'll kill you first!"

Almost of their own volition his hands slid up and around her throat and she sank to her knees choking. Morgan got to his feet, dazed. He staggered forward, grabbed Faulkner by the hair and pulled hard. Faulkner gave a cry of pain, releasing his grip on the woman's throat. As he turned, Morgan picked up the jug of ice water that stood on the bar top and tossed the contents into his face.

The shock seemed to restore Faulkner to his senses. He stood there swaying, an almost vacant look on his face and Morgan went to Joanna and helped her to her feet.

"Are you all right?"

She nodded, without speaking. Morgan turned on Faulkner. "Was that the way it happened, Bruno? Was that how you killed her?"

Faulkner faced them, dangerously calm. His laughter, when it came, was harsh, completely unexpected.

"All right—that's what you've been waiting to

hear, isn't it? Well, let's tell the whole bloody world about it."

He picked up a chair, lifted it high above his head and hurled it through the studio window.

Miller hammered on the door and it was opened almost immediately by Jack Morgan. Joanna Hartmann was slumped into one of the easy chairs by the fire, sobbing bitterly and Faulkner was standing at the bar pouring himself another drink, his back to the door.

"What happened?" Miller demanded.

Morgan moistened dry lips, but seemed to find difficulty in speaking. "Why don't you tell him, Jack?" Faulkner called.

He emptied his glass and turned, the old sneer lifting the corner of his mouth. "Jack and I were at school together, Miller—a very old school. The sort of place that has a code. He's finding it awkward to turn informer."

"For God's sake, Bruno, let's get it over with," Morgan said savagely.

"Anything to oblige." Faulkner turned to Miller. "I killed Grace Packard." He held out his wrists. "Who knows, Miller, you might get promoted over this."

Miller nodded slowly. "You're aware of the seriousness of what you're saying?"

"He admitted it to Miss Hartmann and myself before you arrived," Morgan said wearily. He turned to Bruno. "Don't say anything else at this stage, Bruno. You don't need to."

"I'll have to ask you to accompany me to Central C.I.D. Headquarters," Miller said.

He delivered a formal caution, produced his handcuffs and snapped them over Faulkner's wrists. Faulkner smiled. "You enjoyed doing that, didn't you?"

"Now and then it doesn't exactly make me cry myself to sleep," Miller took him by the elbow.

"I'll come with you if I may," Morgan said..

Faulkner smiled briefly, looking just for that single instant like an entirely different person, perhaps that other self he might have been had things been different.

"It's nice to know one's friends. I'd be obliged, Jack."

"Will Miss Hartmann be all right?" Miller asked.

She looked up, her eyes swollen from weeping and nodded briefly. "Don't worry about me. Will you come back for me, Jack?"

"I'll leave you my car." He dropped the keys on top of the bar.

"Nothing to say, Joanna?" Faulkner demanded.

She turned away, her shoulders shaking and he started to laugh. Miller turned him round, gave him a solid push out on to the landing and Morgan closed the door on the sound of that terrible weeping.

19

It was quiet in the Interrogation Room. The constable at the door picked his nose impassively and thunder sounded again in the distance, a little nearer this time. Harold held the mug of tea in both hands and lifted it to his lips. It was almost cold, the surface covered by a kind of unpleasant scum that filled him with disgust. He shuddered and put the mug down on the table.

"How much longer?" he demanded and the door opened.

Mallory moved to the window and stood there staring out into the rain. Wade positioned himself at the other end of the table and waited, the trousers neatly folded over one arm.

Harold was aware of a strange, choking sensation in his throat. He wrenched at his collar and glanced appealingly at Brady who had closed the door after the constables had discreetly withdrawn. The big Irishman looked troubled. He held Harold's glance for only a moment, then dropped his gaze.

"What did you do with the tenner?" Mallory asked without turning round.

"Tenner? What tenner?" Harold said.

Mallory turned to face him. "The ten-pound note the girl had in her stocking top—what did you do with it?"

"I've never handled a ten-pound note in my life."

"If you'd had any sense you'd have destroyed it, but not you." Mallory carried on as if there had been no interruption. "Where would you change it at that time of night—a pub? Or what about the station buffet—you said you were there."

The flesh seemed to shrink visibly on Harold's bones. "What the hell are you trying to prove?"

Mallory picked up the phone and rang through to the C.I.D. general office. "Mallory here," he told the Duty Inspector. "I want you to get in touch with the manager of the buffet at the Central Station right away. Find out if anyone changed a ten-pound note last night. Yes, that's right—a ten-pound note."

Harold's eyes burned in a face that was as white as paper. "You're wasting your time." He was suddenly belligerent again. "They could have had half a dozen ten-pound notes through their hands on a Saturday night for all you know, so what does it prove?"

"We'll wait and see shall we?"

Harold seemed to pull himself together. He sat straighter in his chair and took a deep breath. "All right, I've had enough. If you're charging me, I want a lawyer. If you're not, then I'm not staying here another minute."

"If you'll extend that to five I'll be more than satisfied," Mallory said.

Harold stared at him blankly. "What do you mean?"

"I'm expecting a chap from the lab to arrive any second. We just want to give you a simple blood test."

"Blood test? What for?"

Mallory nodded to Wade who laid the trousers on the table. "The tests the lab ran on these trousers proved you were with a woman last night."

"All right—I admitted that."

"And the post-mortem on Grace Packard indicated she'd had intercourse with someone just before she died."

"It wasn't with me, that's all I know."

"We can prove that one way or the other with the simplest of tests." It was from that point on that Mallory started to bend the facts. "I don't know if you're aware of it, but it's possible to test a man's semen for his blood group factor."

"So what?"

"During the post-mortem on Grace Packard a semen smear was obtained. It's since been tested in the lab and indicates a certain blood group. When the technician gets here from the lab he'll be able to take a small sample of your blood and tell us what your group is within a couple of minutes—or perhaps you know already?"

Harold stared wildly at him and the silence which enveloped them all was so heavy that suddenly it seemed almost impossible to breathe. His head moved slightly from side to side faster and faster. He tried to get up and then collapsed completely, falling across the table.

He hammered his fist up and down like a hysterical child. "The bitch, the rotten stinking bitch. She shouldn't have laughed at me! She shouldn't have laughed at me!"

He started to cry and Mallory stood there, hands braced against the table, staring down at him. There was a time when this particular moment would have meant something, but not now. In fact, not for some considerable time now.

Quite suddenly the whole thing seemed desperately unreal—a stupid charade that had no substance. It didn't seem to be important any longer and that didn't make sense. Too much in too short a time. Perhaps what he needed was a spot of leave.

He straightened and there was a knock at the door. Brady opened it and a constable handed him a slip of paper. He passed it to Mallory who read it, face impassive. He crumpled it up in one hand and tossed it into the waste bin.

"A message from Dr. Das. Mrs. Phillips died peacefully in her sleep fifteen minutes ago. Thank God for that anyway."

"It would be easy to say I told you so, Miller, but there it is," Mallory said.

Miller took a deep breath. "No possibility of error, sir?"

"None at all. He's given us a full statement. It seems he waited outside Faulkner's flat, saw Faulkner and the girl go in and followed her when she came out. He pulled her into Dob Court where they had some kind of reconciliation because she allowed him to have intercourse with her and she gave him the ten-pound note."

"What went wrong?"

"God alone knows—I doubt if we'll ever get a clear picture. Apparently there was some sort of argument to do with Faulkner and the money. I get the impression that after the way he had treated him, Phillips objected to the idea that Faulkner might have had his way with the girl. The money seemed to indicate that he had."

"So he killed her?"

"Apparently she taunted him, there was an argument and he started to hit her. Lost his temper completely. Didn't mean to kill her of course. They never do."

"Do you think a jury might believe that?"

"With his background? Not in a month of Sundays." The telephone rang. Mallory picked up the receiver, listened for a moment, then put it down. "Another nail in the coffin. It seems the manager of the station buffet has turned up the assistant who changed that ten-pound note last night. Seems she can identify Phillips. He was a regular customer. She says he was in there about a quarter to eleven."

"The bloody fool," Miller said.

"They usually are, Miller, and a good thing for us, I might add."

"But what on earth is Faulkner playing at? I don't understand."

"Let's have him in and find out shall we?"

Mallory sat back and started to fill his pipe. Miller opened the door and called and Faulkner came in followed by Jack Morgan.

Faulkner looked as if he didn't have a care in the world. He stood in front of the desk, trenchcoat draped from his shoulders like a cloak, hands pushed negligently into his pockets.

Mallory busied himself with his pipe. When it was going to his satisfaction, he blew out the match and looked up. "Mr. Faulkner, I have here a full and complete confession to the murder of Grace Packard signed by Harold Phillips. What have you got to say to that?"

"Only that it would appear that I must now add a gift for prophecy to the list of my virtues," Faulkner said calmly.

Morgan came forward quickly. "Is this true, Superintendent?"

"It certainly is. We've even managed to turn up the ten-pound note your client gave the girl. Young Phillips changed it at the station buffet before going home."

Morgan turned on Faulkner, his face white and strained. "What in the hell have you been playing at, for God's sake? You told us that you killed Grace Packard."

"Did I?" Faulkner shrugged. "The other way about as I remember it. You told me." He turned to Mallory. "Mr. Morgan, like all lawyers, Superintendent, has a tendency to believe his own arguments. Once he'd made up his mind I was the nigger in the woodpile, he couldn't help but find proof everywhere he looked."

"Are you trying to say you've just been playing the bloody fool as usual?" Morgan pulled him round angrily. "Don't you realise what you've done to Joanna?"

"She had a choice. She could have believed in me. She took your road." Faulkner seemed completely unconcerned. "I'm sure you'll be very happy together. Can I go now, Superintendent?"

"I think that might be advisable," Mallory said.

Faulkner turned in the doorway, the old sneer lifting the corner of his mouth as he glanced at Miller. "Sorry about that promotion—better luck next time."

After he had gone there was something of a silence. Morgan just stood there, staring wildly into space. Quite suddenly he turned and rushed out without a word.

Miller stood at the window for a long moment, staring down into the rain. He saw Faulkner come out of the main entrance and go down the steps. He paused at the bottom to button his trenchcoat, face lifted to the rain, then walked rapidly away. Morgan appeared a moment later. He watched Faulkner go then hailed a taxi from the rank across thc street.

Miller took out his wallet, produced a pound note and laid it on Mallory's desk. "I was wrong," he said simply.

Mallory noddcd. "You were, but I won't hold that against you. In my opinion Faulkner's probably just about as unbalanced as it's possible to be and still walk free. He'd impair anyone's judgement."

"Nice of you to put it that way, but I was still wrong."

"Never mind." Mallory stood up and reached for his coat. "If you can think of anywhere decent that will still be open on a Sunday afternoon I'll buy you a late lunch out of my ill-gotten gains."

"Okay, sir. Just give me ten minutes to clear my desk and I'm your man."

* * *

The rain was falling heavier than ever as they went down the steps of the Town Hall to the Mini-Cooper. Miller knew a restaurant that might fit the bill, an Italian place that had recently opened in one of the northern suburbs of the city and he drove past the infirmary and took the car through the maze of slum streets behind it towards the new Inner Ring Road.

The streets were deserted, washed clean by the heavy rain and the wipers had difficulty in keeping the screen clear. They didn't speak and Miller drove on mechanically so stunned by what had happened that he was unable to think straight.

They turned a corner and Mallory gripped his arm. "For God's sake, what's that?"

Miller braked instinctively. About half-way along the street, two men struggled beside a parked motorcycle. One of them was a police patrolman in heavy belted stormcoat and black crash helmet. The other wore only shirt and pants and seemed to be barefooted.

The policeman went down, the other man jumped for the motorcycle and kicked it into life. It roared away from the kerb as the patrolman scrambled to his feet, and came straight down the middle of the street. Miller swung the wheel, taking the Mini-Cooper across in an attempt to cut him off. The machine skidded wildly as the rider wrenched the wheel, and shaved the bonnet of the Mini-Cooper with a foot to spare, giving Miller a clear view of his wild, determined face. *Gunner Doyle*. Well this was something he *could* handle. He took the Mini-Cooper round in a full circle across the footpath, narrowly missing an old gas lamp, and went after him.

It was at that precise moment that Jack Morgan arrived back at Faulkner's flat. He knocked on the door and it was opened almost at once by Joanna Hartmann. She was very pale, her eyes swollen from weeping, but seemed well in control of herself. She had a couple of dresses over one arm.

"Hello, Jack, I'm just getting a few of my things together."

That she had lived with Faulkner on occasions was no surprise to him. She moved away and he said quickly, "He didn't kill Grace Packard, Joanna."

She turned slowly. "What did you say?"

"The police had already charged the girl's boy friend when we got there. They have a full confession and corroborating evidence."

"But Bruno said . . ."

Her voice trailed away and Morgan put a hand on her arm gently. "I know what he said, Joanna, but it wasn't true. He was trying to teach us some sort of lesson. He seemed to find the whole thing rather funny."

"He doesn't change, does he?"

"I'm afraid not."

"Where is he now?"

"He went out ahead of me. Last I saw he was going for a walk in the rain."

She nodded briefly. "Let's get out of here then—just give me a moment to get the rest of my things."

"You don't want to see him?"

"Never again."

There was a hard finality in her voice and she turned and went into the bedroom. Morgan followed and stood in the entrance watching. She laid her clothes across the bed and added one or two items which she took from a drawer in one of the dressing tables.

There was a fitted wardrobe against the wall, several suitcases piled on top. She went across and reached up in vain.

"Let me," Morgan said.

He grabbed the handle of the case which was bottom of the pile and eased it out. He frowned suddenly. "Feels as if there's something in it."

He put the case on the bed, flicked the catches and

opened the lid. Inside there was a black plastic handbag, a silk headscarf, a nylon stocking and a high-heeled shoe.

Joanna Hartmann started to scream.

20

Strange, but it was so narrowly avoiding Miller in the park which finally made the Gunner's mind up for him, though not straight away. He waited until the detective had disappeared before emerging from the rhododendron bushes, damp and uncomfortable, his stomach hollow and empty.

He moved away in the opposite direction and finally came to another entrance to the park. Beyond the wrought-iron gate he noticed some cigarette machines. He found the necessary coins from the money Jenny had given him, extracted a packet of ten cigarettes and a book of matches and went back into the park.

He started to walk again, smoking continuously, one cigarette after the other, thinking about everything that had happened since his dash from the infirmary, but particularly about Jenny. He remembered the first time he had seen her from the loft, looking just about as good as a woman could. And the other things. Her ironic humour, her courage in a difficult situation, even the rough edge of her tongue. And when they had made love she had given every part of herself, holding nothing back—something he had never experienced in his life before. *And never likely to again . . .*

The thought pulled him up short and he stood there in the rain contemplating an eternity of being on his own for the first time in his life. Always to be running, always to be afraid because that was the cold fact of it. Scratching for a living, bedding with tarts, sinking fast all the time until someone turned him in for whatever it was worth.

The coppers never let go, never closed a case, that was the trouble. He thought of Miller. It was more than an hour since the detective had walked past the shelter and yet at the memory, the Gunner felt the same panic clutching at his guts, the same instinct to run and keep on running. *Well, to hell with that for a game of soldiers.* Better to face what there was to face and get it over than live like this. There was one cigarette left in the packet. He lit it, tossed the packet away and started to walk briskly towards the other side of the park.

A psychologist would have told him that making a definite decision, choosing a course of action, had resolved his conflict situation. The Gunner would have wondered what in the hell he was talking about. All he knew was that for some unaccountable reason he was cheerful again. One thing was certain—he'd give the bastards something to think about.

On the other side of the park he plunged into the maze of back streets in which he had been hunted during the previous night and worked his way towards the infirmary. It occurred to him that it might be fun to turn up in the very room from which he had disappeared. But there were certain precautions to take first, just to make certain that the police could never link him with Jenny and her grandmother.

A few streets away from the infirmary he stopped in a back alley at a spot where houses were being demolished as fast as the bulldozers could knock them down. On the other side of a low wall, a beck that was little more than a fast-flowing stream of filth rushed past and plunged into a dark tunnel that took it down into the darkness of the city's sewage system.

He took off the raincoat, sweater, boots and socks and dropped them in. They disappeared into the tunnel and he emptied his pockets. Three pound notes and a handful of change. The notes went fluttering down followed by the coins—all but a sixpenny piece. There was a telephone box at the end of the street . . .

He stood in the box and waited as the bell rang at the other end, shivering slightly as the cold struck into his bare feet and rain dripped down across his face. When she answered he could hardly get the coin into the slot for excitement.

"Jenny? It's the Gunner. Is anyone there?"

"Thank God," she said, relief in her voice. "Where are you?"

"A few hundred yards from the infirmary. I'm turning myself in, Jenny. I thought you might like to know that."

"Oh, Gunner." He could have sworn she was crying, but that was impossible. She wasn't the type.

"What about the police?" he asked.

"No one turned up."

"No one turned up?" he said blankly.

A sudden coldness touched his heart, something

elemental, but before he could add anything Jenny said, "Just a minute, Gunner, there's someone outside in the yard now."

A moment later the line went dead.

"You fool," the Gunner said aloud. "You stupid bloody fool."

Why on earth hadn't he seen it before? Only one person could possibly have known he was at the house and it certainly wasn't Ogden who hadn't even seen his face. But the other man had, the one who had attacked Jenny outside the door in the yard.

The Gunner left the phone box like a greyhound erupting from the trap and went down the street on the run. He turned the corner and was already some yards along the pavement when he saw the motorcycle parked at the kerb half-way along. The policeman who was standing beside it was making an entry in his book.

The policeman glanced up just before the Gunner arrived and they met breast-to-breast. There was the briefest of struggles before the policeman went down and the Gunner swung a leg over the motorcycle and kicked the starter.

He let out the throttle too fast so that the machine skidded away from the kerb, front wheel lifting. It was only then that he became aware of the Mini-Cooper at the other end of the street. As he roared towards it, the little car swung broadside on to block his exit. The Gunner threw the bike over so far that the footrest brought sparks from the cobbles, and shaved the bonnet of the Mini-Cooper. For a brief, timeless moment he looked into Miller's face, then he was away.

In the grey afternoon and the heavy rain it was impossible to distinguish the features of the man in the yard at any distance and at first Jenny thought it must be Ogden. Even when the telephone went dead she felt no panic. It was only when she pressed her face to the window and saw Faulkner turn from the wall no more than a yard away, a piece of the telephone line still in his right hand that fear seized her by the throat. She recognised him instantly as her attacker of the previous night and in that moment everything fell neatly into place. The mysterious telephone call, the threat of the police who had never come—all to get rid of the only man who could have protected her.

"Oh, Gunner, God help me now." The words rose in her throat, almost choking her as she turned and stumbled into the hall.

The outside door was still locked and bolted. The handle turned slowly and there was a soft, discreet knocking. For a moment her own fear left her as she remembered the old woman who still lay in bed, her Sunday habit. Whatever happened she must be protected.

Ma Crowther lay propped against the pillows, a shawl around her shoulders as she read one of her regular half-dozen Sunday newspapers. She glanced up in surprise as the door opened and Jenny appeared.

"You all right, Gran?"

"Yes, love, what is it?"

"Nothing to worry about. I just want you to stay in here for a while, that's all."

There was a thunderous knocking from below. Jenny quickly extracted the key on the inside of her grandmother's door, slammed it shut and locked it as the old woman called out to her in alarm.

The knocking on the front door had ceased, but as she went down the stairs, there was the sound of breaking glass from the living-room. When she looked in he was smashing the window methodically with an old wooden clothes prop from the yard. She closed the door of the room, locked it on the outside and went up to the landing.

Her intention was quite clear. When he broke through the flimsy interior door, which wouldn't take long, she would give him a sight of her and then run for the roof. If she could climb across to the metalworks and get down the fire escape there might still be a chance. In any case, she would have led him away from her grandmother.

The door suddenly burst outwards with a great splintering crash and Bruno Faulkner came through with it, fetching up against the opposite wall. He looked up at her for a long moment, his face grave, and started to unbutton his raincoat. He tossed it to one side and put his foot on the bottom step. There was an old wooden chair on the landing. Jenny picked it up and hurled it down at him. He ducked and it missed him, bouncing from the wall.

He looked up at her still calm and then howled like an animal, smashing the edge of his left hand hard against the wooden banister rail. The rail snapped in half, a sight so incredible that she screamed for the first time in her life.

She turned and ran along the landing to the second staircase and Faulkner went after her. At the top of the stairs she was delayed for a moment as she wrestled with the bolt on the door that led to the roof. As she got it open, he appeared at the bottom.

She ran out into the heavy rain, kicked off her shoes and started up the sloping roof, her stocking feet slipping on the wet tiles. She was almost at the top when she slipped back to the bottom. Again she tried, clawing desperately towards the ridge riles as Faulkner appeared from the stairway.

She stuck half-way and stayed here, spread-eagled, caught like a fly on paper. And he knew it, that terrible man below. He came forward slowly and stood there looking up at her. And then he laughed and it was the coldest laugh she had ever heard in her life.

He started forward and the Gunner came through the door like a thunderbolt. Faulkner turned, swerved like a ballet dancer and sent him on his way with a back-handed blow that caught him across the shoulders. The Gunner lost his balance, went sprawling, rolled beneath the rail at the far end and went down the roof that sloped to the yard below.

The Gunner skidded to a halt outside Crowther's yard and dropped the motorcycle on its side no more than four or five minutes after leaving the phone box. He went for the main gate on the run and disappeared through the judas as the Mini-Cooper turned the corner.

It was Mallory who went after him first, mainly because he already had his door open when Miller was still braking, but there was more to it than that.

For some reason he felt alive again in a way he hadn't done for years. It was just like it used to be in the old days as a young probationer in Tower Bridge Division working the docks and the Pool of London. A punch-up most nights and on a Saturday anything could happen and usually did.

The years slipped away from him as he went through the judas on the run in time to see the Gunner scrambling through the front window. Mallory went after him, stumbling over the wreckage of the door on his way into the hall.

He paused for a brief moment, aware of the Gunner's progress above him and went up the stairs quickly. By the time he reached the first landing, his chest was heaving and his mouth had gone bone dry as he struggled for air, but nothing on earth was going to stop him now.

As he reached the bottom of the second flight of stairs, the Gunner went through the open door at the top. A moment later there was a sudden sharp cry. Mallory was perhaps half-way up the stairs when the girl started to scream.

Faulkner had her by the left ankle and was dragging her down the sloping roof when Mallory appeared. In that single moment the whole thing took on every aspect of some privileged nightmare. His recognition of Faulkner was instantaneous, and at the same moment, a great many facts he had refused to face previously, surfaced. As the girl screamed again, he charged.

In his day George Mallory had been a better than average rugby forward and for one year Metropolitan Police light–heavyweight boxing champion. He grabbed Faulkner by the shoulder, pulled him around and swung the same right cross that had earned him his title twenty-seven years earlier. It never even landed. Faulkner blocked the punch, delivered a forward elbow strike that almost paralysed Mallory's breathing system and snapped his left arm like a rotten branch with one devastating blow with the edge of his right hand. Mallory groaned and went down. Faulkner grabbed him by the scruff of the neck and started to drag him along the roof towards the railing.

For Miller it was as if somehow all this had happened before. As he came through the door and paused, thunder split the sky apart overhead and the rain increased into a solid grey curtain that filled the air with a strange, sibilant rushing sound and reduced visibility to a few yards.

He took in everything in a single moment. The girl

with her dress half-ripped from her body, crouched at the foot of the sloping roof crying hysterically, and Faulkner who had now turned to look towards the door, still clutching Mallory's coat collar in his right hand.

Faulkner. A strange fierce exhilaration swept through Miller, a kind of release of every tension that had knotted up inside him during the past twenty-four hours. A release that came from knowing that he had been right all along.

He moved in on the run, jumped high in the air and delivered a flying front kick, the devastating mae-tobigeri, full into Faulkner's face, one of the most crushing of all karate blows. Faulkner staggered back, releasing his hold on Mallory, blood spurting from his mouth and Miller landed awkwardly, slipping in the rain and falling across Mallory.

Before he could scramble to his feet, Faulkner had him by the throat. Miller summoned every effort of will-power and spat full in the other man's face. Faulkner recoiled in a kind of reflex action and Miller stabbed at his exposed throat with stiffened fingers.

Faulkner went back and Miller took his time over getting up, struggling for air. It was a fatal mistake for a blow which would have demolished any ordinary man had only succeeded in shaking Faulkner's massive strength. As Miller straightened, Faulkner moved in like the wind and delivered a fore-fist punch, knuckles extended, that fractured two ribs like matchwood and sent Miller down on one knee with a cry of agony.

Faulkner drew back his foot and kicked him in the stomach. Miller went down flat on his face. Faulkner lifted his foot to crush the skull and Jenny Crowther staggered forward and clutched at his arm. He brushed her away as one might a fly on a summer's day and turned back to Miller. It was at that precise moment that the Gunner reappeared.

The Gunner's progress down the sloping roof had been checked by the presence of an ancient Victorian cast-iron gutter twice the width of the modern variety. He had hung there for some time contemplating the cobbles of the yard thirty feet below. Like Jenny in a similar situation, he had found progress up a steeply sloping bank of Welsh slate in heavy rain a hazardous undertaking. He finally reached for the rusting railings above his head and pulled himself over in time to see Faulkner hurl the girl from him and turn to Miller.

The Gunner, silent on bare feet, delivered a left and a right to Faulkner's kidneys that sent the big man staggering forward with a scream of pain. As he turned, the Gunner stepped over Miller and let Faulkner have his famous left arm screw punch under the ribs followed by a right to the jaw, a combination that had finished no fewer than twelve of his professional fights inside the distance.

Faulkner didn't go down, but he was badly rattled. "Come on then, you bastard," the Gunner yelled. "Let's be having you."

Miller pushed himself up on one knee and tried to lift Mallory into a sitting position. Jenny Crowther crawled across to help and pillowed Mallory's head against her shoulder. He nodded, face twisted in pain, unable to speak and Miller folded his arms tightly about his chest and coughed as blood rose into his mouth.

There had been a time when people had been glad to pay as much as fifty guineas to see Gunner Doyle in action, but up there on the roof in the rain, Miller, the girl and Mallory had a ringside seat for free at his last and greatest battle.

He went after Faulkner two-handed, crouched like a tiger. Faulkner was hurt—hurt badly, and the Gunner had seen enough to know that his only chance lay in keeping him in that state. He swayed to one side as Faulkner threw a punch and smashed his left into the exposed mouth that was already crushed and bleeding from Miller's efforts. Faulkner cried out in pain and the Gunner gave him a right that connected just below the eye and moved close.

"Keep away from him," Miller yelled. "Don't get too close."

The Gunner heard only the roar of the crowd as he breathed in the stench of the ring—that strange never-to-be-forgotten compound of human sweat, heat, and embrocation. He let Faulkner have another right to the jaw to straighten him up and stepped in close for a blow to the heart that might finish the job. It was his biggest mistake. Faulkner pivoted, delivering an elbow strike backwards that doubled the Gunner over. In the same moment Faulkner turned again, lifting the Gunner backwards with a knee in the face delivered with such force that he went staggering across the roof and fell heavily against the railing. It sagged, half-breaking and he hung there trying to struggle to his feet, blood pouring from his nose and mouth. Faulkner charged in like a runaway express train, shoulder down and sent him back across the railing. The Gunner rolled over twice on the way down, bounced across the broad iron gutter and fell to the cobbles below.

Faulkner turned slowly, a terrifying sight, eyes glaring, blood from his mouth soaking down into his collar. He snarled at the three of them helpless before him, grabbed at the sagging iron railing and wrenched a four-foot length of it free. He gave a kind of animal-like growl and started forward.

Ma Crowther stepped through the door at the head of the stairs, still in her nightdress, clutching her sawn-off shotgun against her breast. Faulkner didn't see her, so intent was he on the task before him. He poised over his three victims, swinging the iron bar high above his head like an executioner, and she gave him both barrels full in the face.

21

It was almost nine o'clock in the evening when Miller and Jenny Crowther walked along the second floor corridor of the Marsden Wing of the General Infirmary towards the room in which they had put Gunner Doyle.

They walked slowly because Miller wasn't in any fit state to do anything else. His body seemed to be bruised all over and he was strapped up so tightly because of his broken ribs that he found breathing difficult. He was tired. A hell of a lot had happened since that final terrible scene on the roof and with Mallory on his back, he had been the only person capable of handling what needed to be done. A series of pain-killing injections weren't helping any and he was beginning to find difficulty in thinking straight any more.

The constable on the chair outside the door stood up and Miller nodded familiarly. "Look after Miss Crowther for a few minutes will you, Harry? I want a word with the Gunner."

The policeman nodded, Miller opened the door and went in. There was a screen on the other side of the door and beyond it the Gunner lay propped against the pillows, his nose broken for the fourth time in his life, his right leg in traction, fractured in three places.

Jack Brady sat in a chair on the far side of the bed reading his notebook. He got up quickly. "I've got a statement from him. He insists that he forced his way into the house last night; that Miss Crowther and her grandmother only allowed him to stay under duress."

"Is that a fact?" Miller looked down at the Gunner and shook his head. "You're a poor liar, Gunner. The girl's already given us a statement that clarifies the entire situation. She says that when you saved her from Faulkner in the yard, she and her grandmother felt that they owed you something. She seems to think that's a good enough defence even in open court."

"What do you think?" the Gunner said weakly.

"I don't think it will come to court so my views don't count. You put up the fight of your life back there on the roof. Probably saved our lives."

"Oh, get stuffed," the Gunner said. "I want to go to sleep."

"Not just yet. I've got a visitor for you."

"Jenny?" The Gunner shook his head. "I don't want to see her."

"She's been waiting for hours."

"What in the hell does she want to see me for? There's nothing to bleeding well say, is there? I'll lose all my remission over this little lot. I'm going back to the nick for another two and a half years plus anything else the beak likes to throw at me for the things I've done while I've been out. On top of that I'll be dragging this leg around behind me like a log of wood for the rest of my life when I get out."

"And a bloody good thing as well," Brady said brutally. "No more climbing for you, my lad."

"I'll get her now," Miller said. "You can see her alone. We'll wait outside."

The Gunner shrugged. "Suit yourself."

Miller and Brady went out and a second later, the girl came round the screen and stood at the end of the bed. Her face was very pale and there was a nasty bruise on her forehead, but she was still about fifty times better in every possible way than any other woman he'd ever met. There was that strange choking feeling in his throat again. He was tired and in great pain. He was going back to gaol for what seemed like forever and for the first time he was afraid of the prospect. He felt just like a kid who had been hurt. He wanted to have her come round the bed and kiss him, smooth back his hair, pillow his head on her shoulder.

But that was no good—no good at all. What he did now was the most courageous thing he had ever done in his entire life, braver by far than his conduct on the roof when facing Faulkner.

He smiled brightly. "Surprise, surprise. What's all this?"

"I've been waiting for hours. They wouldn't let me in before. Gran sends her regards."

"How is she?" The Gunner couldn't resist the question. "They tell me she finished him off good and proper up there. How's she taken it? Flat on her back?"

"Not her—says she'd do it again any day. They've told you who he was?" The Gunner nodded and she went on, "I was in such a panic when he started smashing his way in that I locked her in the bedroom and forgot all about the shotgun. She keeps it in the wardrobe. She had to shoot the lock off to get out."

"Good job she arrived when she did from what they tell me."

There was a slight silence and she frowned. "Is anything wrong, Gunner?"

"No—should there be?"

"You seem funny, that's all."

"That's me all over, darlin'. To tell you the truth I was just going to get some shut-eye when you turned up."

Her face had gone very pale now. "What is it, Gunner? What are you trying to say?"

"What in the hell am I supposed to say?" He snapped back at her, genuinely angry. "Here I am flat on my back like a good little lad. In about another month they'll stick me in a big black van and take me back where I came from. That's what you wanted, isn't it?"

She had gone very still. "I thought it was what *you* wanted—really wanted."

"And how in the hell would you know what I want?"

"I've been about as close to you as any woman could get and . . ."

He cut in sharply with a laugh that carried just the

right cutting edge to it. "Do me a favour, darlin'. No bird gets close to me. Just because I've had you between the sheets doesn't mean I've sold you the rights to the story of my life for the Sunday papers. It was very nice—don't get me wrong. You certainly know what to do with it, but I've got other fish to fry now."

She swayed. For a moment it seemed as if she might fall and then she turned and went out. The Gunner closed his eyes. He should have felt noble. He didn't. He felt sick and afraid and more alone than he had ever done in his life before.

The girl was crying when she came out of the room. She kept on going, head-down and Miller went after her. He caught her, swung her round and shoved her against the wall.

"What happened in there?"

"He made it pretty clear what he really thinks about me, that's all," she said. "Can I go now?"

"Funny how stupid intelligent people can be sometimes," Miller shook his head wearily. "Use your head, Jenny. When he left your house he was wearing shoes and a raincoat, had money in his pocket—money you'd given him. Why did he telephone you?"

"To say he was giving himself up."

"Why was he barefooted again? Why had he got rid of the clothes you gave him? Why did he come running like a bat out of hell when you were in danger?"

She stared at him, eyes wide and shook her head. "But he was rotten in there—he couldn't have done more if he'd spat on me."

"Exactly the result he was hoping for, can't you see that?" Miller said gently. "The biggest proof of how much he thinks of you is the way he's just treated you." He took her arm. "Let's go back inside. You stay behind the screen and keep your mouth shut and I'll prove it to you."

The Gunner was aware of the click of the door opening, there was a soft footfall and he opened his eyes and looked up at Miller. "What do you want now, copper?"

"Congratulations," Miller said. "You did a good job—on the girl, I mean. Stupid little tart like that deserves all she gets."

It was all it took. The Gunner tried to sit up, actually tried to get at him. "You dirty bastard. She's worth ten of you—any day of the week. In my book you aren't fit to clean her shoes."

"Neither are you."

"The only difference between us is I know it. Now get to hell out of here and leave me alone."

He closed his eyes as Miller turned on heel and limped out. The door clicked and there was only the silence. He heard no sound and yet something seemed to move and then there was the perfume very close.

He opened his eyes and found her bending over him. "Oh, Gunner," she said. "Whatever am I going to do with you?"

Miller sat on the end of Mallory's bed to make his report. The Chief Superintendent had a room to himself in the private wing as befitted his station. There were already flowers in the corner and his wife was due to arrive within the hour.

"So you've left them together?" Mallory said.

Miller nodded. "He isn't going to run anywhere."

"What about the leg? How bad is it?"

"Not too good, according to the consultant in charge. He'll be lame for the rest of his life. It could have been worse, mind you."

"No more second-storey work at any rate," Mallory commented.

"Which could make this injury a blessing in disguise," Miller pointed out.

Mallory shook his head. "I hardly think so. Once a thief always a thief and Doyle's a good one—up there with the best. Clever, resourceful, hightly intelligent. When you think of it, he hasn't done anything like the time he should have considering what he's got away with in the past. He'll find something else that's just as crooked, mark my words."

Which was probably true, but Miller wasn't going down without a fight. "On the other hand if he hadn't been around last night Jenny Crowther would have been number five on Faulkner's list and we'd have been no further forward. I'd also like to point out that we'd have been in a damn bad way without him up there on the roof."

"Which is exactly how the newspapers and the great British public will see it, Miller," Mallory said. "You needn't flog it to death. As a matter of interest I've already dictated a report for the Home Secretary in which I state that in my opinion Doyle had earned any break we can give him."

Miller's tiredness dropped away like an old cloak. "What do you think that could mean—a pardon?"

Mallory laughed out loud. "Good God, no. If he's lucky, they'll release him in ten months on probation as they would have done anyway if he hadn't run for it."

"Fair enough, sir."

"No, it isn't, Miller. He'll be back. You'll see."

"I'm putting my money on Jenny Crowther." Miller got to his feet. "I'd better go now, sir. You look as if you could do with some sleep."

"And you look as if you might fall down at any moment." Miller turned, a hand on the door and Mallory called, "Miller?"

"Yes, sir?"

"Regarding that little wager of ours. I was right about Phillips—he killed Grace Packard just as I said, but taking everything else into consideration I've decided to give you your pound back, and no arguments."

He switched off the light with his good hand and Miller went out, closing the door softly behind him.

He took the lift down to the entrance hall and found Jack Brady standing outside the night sister's small glass office talking to her. They turned as Miller came forward and the sister frowned.

"You look awful. You should be in your bed, really you should."

"Is that an invitation, Sister?" Miller demanded and kissed her on the cheek.

Brady tapped out his pipe and slipped a hand under Miller's arm. "Come on, Nick, let's go."

"Go where?"

"The nearest pub. I'd like to see what a large whisky does for you, then I'll take you home."

"You're an Irish gentleman, Jack. God bless you for the kind thought."

They went out through the glass doors. The rain had stopped and Miller took a deep breath of fresh, damp air. "Hell is always today, Jack, never tomorrow. Have you ever noticed that?"

"It's all that keeps a good copper going," Brady said and they went down the steps together.

Turn the page for a shocking preview of

DARK JUSTICE

available in paperback from Berkley
in August 2005.

1

Manhattan on a dark November evening around eight o'clock was bleak and uninviting, an east wind driving heavy rain before it, as Henry Morgan turned the corner of a side street into Park Avenue.

He was a small man wearing a dark blue uniform and cap with the legend ICON SECURITY emblazoned on each shoulder; in one hand was a black leather bag, and the other held an umbrella over his head.

Park Avenue was hardly deserted at that hour, cars swishing by, although there were few pedestrians because of the rain. He turned into a convenient doorway for a moment and looked each way. It was a mixture of offices and residences, mostly impressive town houses, lights at the windows. He'd always loved cities by night and felt a sudden nostalgia, emotional of course, and he took a deep breath. After all, he'd come a long way for this, a long way, and here he was at the final end of things. Time to get on with it. He picked up the bag and stepped out.

A hundred yards farther on, he came to an office building no more than four stories high, a building of some distinction to it, older than the adjacent buildings. There was discreet lighting on the ground floor, obviously for security. A sign in gold leaf on one of the windows said GOULD & COMPANY, BANK DEPOSITORY and indicated business hours from nine until four in the afternoon. He stepped into the arched entrance, peering through the armored plate-glass door into the lighted foyer, and pressed the buzzer for Chesney, only Chesney didn't come. Instead, a large black man wearing the same dark blue uniform appeared and opened the door.

"Hey, you're late. Morgan, isn't it? The English guy? Chesney told me about you."

Morgan stepped inside. The door closed noiselessly behind him. A bad start, but he'd have to make the best of it.

"I'm sorry. I always get Chesney coffee and sandwiches from a place round the corner." He followed the other man through to the reception area. "Where is he?"

"The way I heard it, his gallbladder's playing up again, so they rushed me over from South Street."

"What do I call you?"

"Smith will do." He sat behind the desk, took out a pack of Marlboros and lit one. "A busy night out there, but at least there are a couple of good movies on TV. So you're from London, they tell me?"

"That's right."

"So what are you doing over here?"

"Oh, pastures new, you know how it is."

"Lucky you got a green card."

"Well, I'd been doing this kind of thing over there. It helped."

Smith nodded. "Anyway, let's see what you've got in that bag." Morgan's stomach turned hollow and he hesitated. Smith reached for the bag. "I'm starving, and what with them rushing me over here at the last minute, I had no chance to get anything."

Morgan hurriedly pulled the bag up, put it on the desk, opened it, produced coffee and sandwiches and passed them over.

"What about you?" Smith asked.

"I'll have mine later. I'll do the rounds first."

"Suit yourself." Smith started to unwrap a sandwich.

"I'll get started, then. I'll just drop my bag in the rest room."

He moved to the other end of the foyer and did just that, then called to Smith, "See you later."

"Take your time." Smith switched on the television, and Morgan entered the elevator and pressed the buttons that took him down to the vault.

He checked it thoroughly, giving what he'd put in the coffee time to work, although the effect was almost instantaneous and good for five hours, or so they'd told him. He trawled the vault, hundreds of steel boxes behind bars, went back to the elevator and ascended to the fourth floor.

It was all office accommodation, everything in good order, and it was the same when he went down to the third and then the second floor. Boring, really, to have to spend your working life doing this. But it would soon be over. He returned to the elevator and went down.

* * *

Smith was slumped across the desk, out completely, the partly drunk coffee cup beside him. The sandwich had a couple of bites out of it, but that was all. Morgan shook him to make sure, then turned to the general security box and switched it off for the entire building. He went along to the rest room, retrieved his bag, got into the elevator and went to the second floor.

When he went out, he dimmed the lights, walked across to the window looking out over Park Avenue to the splendid town house on the other side, its many windows ablaze with lights. Parking had been banned for the whole block, and not just because it was owned by Senator Harvey Black.

Having switched off thc entire alarm system, Morgan was able to open the control panel by the window without any unseemly fuss. He started to whistle softly, put the bag on the table, opened it and produced an AK-47, unfolded the stock, cocked it and laid it across the windowsill, checking his watch.

It was twenty to nine and the fund-raiser at the Pierre would just be finishing. Senator Black would be bringing his honored guest back to the house for dinner at nine o'clock.

Morgan took a pack of cigarettes from his pocket, lit one and sat there at the open window, cradling the

AK-47 with every intention of shooting the President of the United States dead the moment he stepped out on the pavement.

Suddenly, he heard the sound of the elevator in operation below. For a moment, he froze in a kind of panic, then jumped to his feet and turned to face the elevator. It stopped and Smith stepped out, followed by a tall, handsome man of fifty or so, black hair graying.

"Why, Henry," Smith said. "What's all this? I didn't see anything about it in the job description."

Morgan backed away, thinking hard.

There was a pause and the other man said, "Mr. Morgan, my name is Blake Johnson. I work for the President of the United States. This gentleman is Clancy Smith of the Secret Service. I regret to tell you that the President isn't coming tonight. Seems he canceled the dinner at the last moment and flew back to Washington. So sorry."

He stepped forward and, in a single motion, Morgan raised the AK and fired at point-blank range—but only the rattle of the bolt sounded.

Smith said, "Forgot to mention. I emptied it when

you went down to the vault. And by the way—I never accept coffee from strangers."

Morgan dropped the AK to the floor with a look of despair on his face. Johnson almost felt sorry for him.

"Hell, man, we got Saddam Hussein. Did you really think *you* could pull this off? Anything to say?"

"Yes," Morgan said. "Beware the Wrath of Allah."

He seemed to bite hard, his jaw tightening, then he staggered back, tripped and fell to the floor, moaning terribly, his face contorted. There was a strange, pungent smell as Smith dropped to one knee and peered closely at him. He glanced up, "I don't know what in the hell that smell is, but this guy is dead."

By special arrangement, Blake had the body removed by army paramedics and conveyed to an exclusive private hospital used mainly for rehab patients. It did, however, offer state-of-the-art morgue facilities and he'd called in one of New York's finest chief medical examiners, Dr. George Romano, to do the necessary.

He and Clancy had stopped off at their hotel so that Clancy could change from the security uniform, and arrived at their destination a good hour after the corpse and found Romano in the Superintendent's office already garbed for action. He and Blake were old friends. Romano had done a lot of work for the Basement, the White House security organization that Johnson ran. Romano was drinking coffee and smoking.

"I thought that was against the law these days, especially for doctors."

"Around here I make my own rules, Blake. Who's your friend?"

"Clancy Smith, Secret Service. He's taken a bullet for the President in the past. Fortunately, nothing like that was needed tonight."

"I've started on our friend, Mr. Morgan. Just taking a break."

"John Doe, if you don't mind," Blake said.

"And what if I do?"

Blake turned to Clancy, who opened the briefcase he carried, took out a document and passed it across to the doctor.

"You'll notice that's addressed to one George Romano and signed by President Jake Cazalet. It's what's called a 'presidential warrant.' It says you belong to the President, it transcends all our laws, and you can't even say no. You also never discuss what happened tonight, because it never happened."

For once, Romano wasn't smiling. "That bad?"

He shook his head. "I should have known when I realized you'd given me a Heinrich Himmler."

"What in the hell is that supposed to mean?" Clancy demanded.

"I'll go back in and show you if you can stand to watch."

"I was in Vietnam and Clancy was in the Gulf. I think we can stand it," Blake said.

"Excuse me, I was in 'Nam, too," said Romano, "and with all due respect, the Gulf War was pussy."

"Yeah, well, Clancy here has got two Navy Crosses to prove otherwise," Blake said. "But let's get on with it."

In the postmortem room, two technicians waited while Romano scrubbed up again. He was helped into surgical gloves and moved to the naked body of Henry Morgan, who lay on the slanting steel table, his head raised high on a wooden block, the mouth gaping. Close at hand were a video recorder and an instrument cart.

Romano said, "Wednesday, November third, resuming postmortem, Henry Morgan, address unknown." He turned to Blake and Clancy. "Come closer. Because of the unusual circumstances, I decided to investigate the mouth first, and if you look closely you'll find a molar missing at the left side."

He pulled the mouth open with a finger and disclosed the bloodied gap.

"And here it is, gents." He picked up a small stainless-steel pan and rattled the crushed remains of a tooth in it that was part gold. "Heinrich Himmler, for the benefit of those too young to remember, was Reichsführer of the SS during the immortal days of the Third Reich. However, he was smart enough to know that all good things come to an end and didn't fancy the hangman's noose. So he had a false tooth fitted that contained a cyanide capsule. A number of Nazis did. Faced with capture, you crunch down as hard as you can. Death is virtually instantaneous."

"So our friend here had no intention of being taken alive?"

"I'd say so. Now, in spite of the fact that I suspect it will prove useless, I intend to complete my usual thorough examination. What, by the way, do you know about the guy?"

"The only thing I can tell you is that he's thirty years old. When can I have the body?"

"I'd say an hour should do it."

"Good. I'll arrange transportation while we're waiting in the office, and George . . ." He pulled him away and murmured softly, "I don't mind the technicians having heard the Himmler bit, but nothing more. No comment. And bring the videotape when you're finished."

"Yes, O great one."

Romano turned back to the task at hand, and Blake and Clancy went out.

They sat in the Superintendent's office, and Blake made a call on his Codex mobile. It was answered almost instantly.

"Highgrove."

"It's Blake Johnson, I phoned earlier about a disposal."

"Of course, sir. We're ready and waiting."

"You know where we are. The package will be ready in one hour."

"We'll be there."

"And I'll expect the disposal to be immediate."

"Naturally."

Blake switched off. "Let's have some coffee."

There was a pot standing ready in the machine. Clancy went and poured two cups. "Not a thing on him. Swept clean. No ID, no passport, and yet he had to have one to get into the country."

"Probably stashed it before he came here tonight. Everything else was likely forged. Came into the country posing as a tourist. A forged green card was supplied, a room booked for him in some modest hotel."

"And the AK?"

"Could have been left for him in a locker anywhere. The job at the security agency could have been arranged for him in advance. I'll bet he didn't even meet anyone from his organization here in New York."

"But some outfit sent him from London."

"Of course, otherwise why would he be here? They've probably got friends in New York who kept an anonymous eye on him, but preferred not to get involved."

"I wouldn't blame them. It was a suicide mission," Clancy said. "Even if we hadn't gotten him now, he'd have been run down like a dog if the worst had happened."

"Very probably. Now I must speak to the President."

He found Cazalet at his desk in the Oval Office.

"Mr. President, we got him. The whole thing was for real. He's dead, unfortunately."

"That is unfortunate. Gunshot wound?"

"Cyanide."

"Dear me. Where are you now?"

"The mortuary, waiting for the disposal team."

"Fine. Take care of it, Blake. This never happened. I don't want it on the front page of the *New York Times*. I'll order a plane to pick up you and Clancy. I want you back here as soon as possible so we can sort things out."

"Yes, Mr. President."

"And since it was our British cousins who alerted us to the existence of Morgan, you'd better telephone General Ferguson and let him know."

In London, it was four o'clock in the morning when the security phone rang at General Charles Ferguson's flat in Cavendish Place. He switched on the bedside light and answered.

"At such an appalling hour, I can only assume this is of supreme importance."

"It always is when it concerns the Empire, Charles."

It was the code word used to indicate the President in danger.

Ferguson was fully alert now and sat up. "Blake, my good friend. What happened?"

"Your information on Henry Morgan was dead-on.

He tried to hit the President tonight, but Clancy and I stopped him. Unfortunately, he had a cyanide tooth, so he's no longer with us."

"Is the President all right?"

"Absolutely. As for Morgan, what's left of him will soon be six pounds of gray ash. I'll probably flush it down the toilet."

"You're a hard man, Blake, harder than I believed possible."

"It's the nature of the job, Charles, and the bastard did intend to assassinate the President. Anyway, thanks to you and the rest of the Prime Minister's Private Army, it's all come out fine. Thank them all for me: Hannah Bernstein, Sean Dillon, and Major Roper."

"Especially Roper on this one. The man's a genius on the computer."

"Got to run, Charles. I'll be in touch."

Blake put the phone down, and Romano entered carrying a videotape and several documents.

"Good man," Blake said.

"Not really." Romano lit a cigarette. "I'm smart enough to know my place, that's all."

Clancy had gone out to check the corridor and found two men in black coats pushing a gurney with a body bag on it.

One of them, a quietly cadaverous man, said, "Mr. Johnson?"

Blake leaned out of the office door. "He's all ready and waiting for you. Load him on and we'll see you at Highgrove. Tell Mr. Coffin to wait until we arrive."

"As you say, sir."

They moved away. Clancy said, "Coffin? Is that for real?"

"If it's the man I know, it certainly is." Romano smiled bleakly. "Fergus Coffin. I believe it's called life imitating art." At that moment, the gurney returned with what was obviously Henry Morgan in the body bag. "On your way now, gentlemen. I think I've had enough for one night."

In the mortuary at Highgrove, Blake and Clancy waited by the ovens. Fergus Coffin and an attendant pushed the gurney forward, the body still enclosed in the black body bag.

Blake said, "Open it."

Coffin nodded and his associate unzipped it, exposing the head. Henry Morgan it was.

"He looks at peace," Blake said.

"He would be, Mr. Johnson," Coffin told him. "Death is a serious business. I've devoted my life to it."

"No questions?"

"None. I've seen the presidential warrant, but it's more than that. You're a good man, Mr. Johnson. Every instinct tells me that. You've known great sorrow."

Blake, remembering a murdered wife, stiffened for a moment and then said, "How long?"

"With the new technology, thirty minutes."

"Then get on with it. Put him in, but I need to see." He held out the documents and video. "And these."

The other man opened one of the oven doors, Coffin pushed the gurney forward, Henry Morgan slid inside. Coffin pulled the gurney away, the glass door closed, a button was pressed. The oven flared at once, the gas jets peaking, and the body bag flared instantly, also the video and documents.

Blake turned to Clancy. "We'll wait," and led the way outside.

In the office, they smoked cigarettes. Clancy said, "You want coffee?"

"Not in a million years. A good stiff drink is what I need, but we'll have to wait until we're on the plane."

Rain hammered against the window. Clancy said, "Does it ever bother you, this kind of thing?"

"Clancy, I went to war for my country in Vietnam

when I was very young and full of ideals. I never really regretted it. Someone had to do it. Now, all these years later, we're at war with the world—a world where global terrorism is the name of the game." He stubbed out his cigarette in an ashtray. "And Clancy, I'll do anything it takes. I took an oath to my President and I take that to be an oath to my country." He smiled slightly. "Does that give you a problem?"

And Clancy Smith, once the youngest sergeant major in the Marine Corps, smiled. "Not in the slightest."

At that moment, the door opened and Coffin entered, holding a plastic urn. "Henry Morgan, six pounds of gray ash."

"Excellent," Blake said, and Clancy took the urn.

"Many thanks," Blake told Coffin. "Believe me, you've never done anything more important."

"I accept your word for that, Mr. Johnson," and Coffin went out.

"Let's go," Blake said, and added, "Bring the urn with you."

He led the way out to the parking lot, where the rain poured down relentlessly. They walked to their limousine, which as parked by what, in season, would obviously be a flower bed.

Blake said, "I was going to put those ashes down

the toilet, but let's be more civilized and do something for the next year's flowers."

"Good idea."

Clancy unscrewed the top of the urn and poured the ashes over the flower bed.

"I believe it's called strewing."

"I don't care what it's called. Washington next, so let's catch that plane."